Powerful and dangerous . . .

A star pendant around Dr. Q's neck sparkled in the light. She sighed deeply. "To be a hypnotist," she said, "one must first be in tune with one's own innermost thoughts and feelings."

"Check," Jessica said, busily writing it down. That's easy. I'm the most in-tune person I know!

"Second," Dr. Q went on, holding up a long finger, "the hypnotist must achieve a state of absolute calm."

"Absolute calm," Jessica wrote. She suspected she might have misspelled absolute, but she didn't care. That'll be easy too, she told herself happily. I'm always calm. She looked up. "But how do you—"

"Hypnosis is an art," Dr. Q went on, rearranging the folds of her skirt. "I can give you some suggestions about developing your skills, but there is one thing you must remember."

"Which is?" Jessica said, wondering when they would get to the good stuff.

"Just this." Dr. Q leaned forward and fixed Jessica with her hardest stare yet. "Hypnosis is not a toy, never a toy. It is a tool, and a powerful but dangerous one." She folded her hands neatly in her lap. "Do not play with it. Do you understand?"

SWEET VALLEY TWINS

The Mysterious Dr. Q

Written by
Jamie Suzanne

Created by
FRANCINE PASCAL

BANTAM BOOKS
NEW YORK · TORONTO · LONDON · SYDNEY · AUCKLAND

To Meris Rose Tombari

RL 4, 008-012

THE MYSTERIOUS DR. Q
A Bantam Book / December 1996

Sweet Valley High® *and Sweet Valley Twins*® *are
registered trademarks of Francine Pascal.*

Conceived by Francine Pascal.

*Produced by Daniel Weiss Associates, Inc.
33 West 17th Street
New York, NY 10011.*

Cover art by James Mathewuse.

ISBN: 0-553-48433-8

Published simultaneously in the United States and Canada

*Bantam Books are published by Bantam Books, a division of Bantam
Doubleday Dell Publishing Group, Inc. Its trademark, consisting of the
words "Bantam Books" and the portrayal of a rooster, is Registered in the
U.S. Patent and Trademark Office and in other countries. Marca
Registrada. Bantam Books, 1540 Broadway, New York, New York 10036.*

PRINTED IN THE UNITED STATES OF AMERICA

OPM   0 9 8 7 6 5 4 3 2 1

One

◇

"What do you know about hypnosis?" Mr. Bowman asked Elizabeth Wakefield. It was Tuesday afternoon, and Elizabeth was in the office of the *Sweet Valley Sixers*, the sixth-grade class newspaper she edited with her friend Amy Sutton.

"Hypnosis?" Elizabeth raised her eyebrows, glad to have a distraction. The next issue of the *Sixers* was due out soon, and Elizabeth was trying hard to think of an interesting article for the front page. "Not much," she admitted. "Why do you ask?"

Mr. Bowman grinned. He was faculty adviser to the newspaper as well as Elizabeth's English teacher. "Tell you in a minute," he said carelessly, returning to his computer keyboard. "Go on back to what you were doing. Sorry to bother you."

Hypnosis? Elizabeth wondered. She shrugged

and focused on the story ideas in front of her. "The kids who were circulating a petition to allow skateboarding in the halls."

No. Elizabeth pushed a strand of hair out of her eyes. She was sure Bruce Patman and the other kids passing the petition would never convince the principal. And anyway, she didn't believe many kids would sign. *It's kind of a dumb idea,* she thought.

Mr. Bowman hummed tunelessly to himself as he tapped away.

Elizabeth scanned the next item on her list: "the latest megahit album from Johnny Buck." Elizabeth nodded slowly. She could get kids' reactions to the songs on the recording. But knowing the students at Sweet Valley Middle School, she'd probably just get the same reaction a million times. Bruce would say, "Awesome!" Amy would say, "Outrageous!" Elizabeth's twin sister, Jessica, would say, "Cool!" Big deal.

Todd Wilkins—now, Todd might have something different to say about the album. Todd didn't always just follow the crowd. He was kind of cute too, and he had a nice personality. Elizabeth smiled as she thought about him. But one sort-of-interesting opinion about the album wouldn't make for much of a newspaper article. Even if the opinion belonged to Todd.

The word *hypnosis* popped into her mind again. Elizabeth sighed. *Great. Now I'll stay awake all night wondering why Mr. Bowman asked me about hypnosis.*

Mr. Bowman's keyboard suddenly went silent, and the office was filled with the sounds of a computer printer. Mr. Bowman swiveled his chair to face Elizabeth. "How about a woman named Dr. Q?" he asked. "Ever heard of her?"

Elizabeth wrinkled her nose. *Dr. Q?* She vaguely remembered some old black-and-white movie on TV about a character named Dr. Q. Or was it Dr. Z? "I don't think so," she said, shaking her head. "Who is she?"

"She's a hypnotist as well as a psychic—" Mr. Bowman adjusted his glasses and looked meaningfully at Elizabeth. "And she's coming here."

"Here?" Elizabeth frowned. "To Sweet Valley?"

"To this school," Mr. Bowman corrected her. Behind him, the printer spewed out a sheet of paper. "She's going to be the speaker at the assembly on Thursday."

Elizabeth blinked. "You mean the day after tomorrow?"

"The day after tomorrow," Mr. Bowman confirmed. "So—what do you know about hypnosis, Elizabeth?"

"Like I said, not much," Elizabeth confessed. "Isn't hypnosis when you make someone do whatever you tell them to do?" She strained to remember the Saturday morning cartoons she'd seen when she was younger. "When you hold up a shiny medallion and swing it back and forth, and your subjects fall asleep and then they're in your power?" Come to think of it, she decided, hypnosis sounded pretty lame.

Mr. Bowman smiled. "Well, not exactly," he explained. He handed her two sheets of paper from the printer tray. "People don't really fall asleep," he went on, "and most experts agree that hypnosis isn't quite that simple anyway."

"Oh." Elizabeth glanced at the top sheet. "'Hypnosis,'" she read aloud. "'Fact or fiction?'"

"It's some background information I'm getting off the Internet," Mr. Bowman explained. He leaned over Elizabeth's shoulder. "Some scientists say that people who perform hypnosis in public, like this Dr. Q person, are frauds. They don't hypnotize anyone, just use tricks to put on a show."

Elizabeth raised her eyebrows. "I think I'd kind of agree with that," she said. An image from one cartoon flashed into her mind: a clown waving a medallion and saying, "Watch the pretty coin of gold, and you will do as you are told." Then the guy who'd been hypnotized had howled at the moon.

"Would you?" Mr. Bowman shrugged. "Other scientists say that hypnosis is something real and powerful, although it's a mysterious force that we can't understand."

Elizabeth couldn't help laughing. "That sounds like something Jessica would say," she told Mr. Bowman. Elizabeth could see her twin now, desperate to be part of Dr. Q's demonstration on Thursday. *It's amazing how different we are*, Elizabeth thought.

On the outside, the twins looked exactly alike. Each had the same long blond hair and the same blue-green eyes. Both were in sixth grade. But the similarities ended there.

Elizabeth loved nothing better than curling up with a good book. She enjoyed working on the newspaper, writing stories, and spending time with a few close friends. Jessica, on the other hand, lived for long discussions about boys, clothes, and soap operas. Most of her energy went into the Unicorn Club, a group of girls who considered themselves the prettiest and most popular in Sweet Valley Middle School. Elizabeth and her friends privately called the Unicorn Club the Snob Squad. In return, Jessica thought that Elizabeth's friends were boring and childish.

And now here was another difference between them, Elizabeth realized. She'd already made up her mind, pretty much, that Dr. Q was a fake. But Jessica—

Elizabeth's eyes twinkled. Jessica was exactly the kind of person who would believe in auras and psychic powers. She'd love the idea of a hypnotist coming to the school.

"Yes, I imagine Jessica might be a true believer," Mr. Bowman remarked. He smiled at Elizabeth. "So I thought you might like to read up on hypnotism. Who knows, maybe you can put together a story on this."

Elizabeth thumbed through the papers Mr. Bowman had given her. "How do they cheat?" she asked.

"Here's one way," Mr. Bowman said. He pointed to a paragraph on the second page. "Seems that some hypnotists tell their subjects that their fingertips are going to taste sweet. Then they get their subjects to touch a book—which they've secretly coated with sugar."

"So of course their fingertips taste sweet!" Elizabeth said slowly. "That's not fair."

Mr. Bowman spread out his hands. "Just remember, other scientists believe there are forces that we don't understand. And many people say that hypnotists help them with problems in their lives—overcoming fears, for instance."

"Yeah, yeah," Elizabeth said, but she was barely listening. An idea was running through her mind.

First she'd watch Dr. Q like a hawk on Thursday. Then she'd schedule an interview with Dr. Q. In Dr. Q's office. A seriously hard-hitting investigative piece. Like the ones Amy Sutton's mom did on TV; Amy's mom was a reporter for one of the local stations. Elizabeth could see the *Sixers* headline now: "Dr. Q a Fraud, Ace Reporter Proves." She'd look for sugar and other sneaky things and—

Elizabeth took a deep breath. "Please get me anything else about hypnosis that you can, Mr. Bowman," she said, drawing an X through the story topics on her list. "We've got a front-page article for the next issue!"

"Patman!" Todd Wilkins shouted. He dribbled sharply away from Ken Matthews, who was guarding him, and sent a perfect bounce pass right into Bruce Patman's hands. *Terrific.* Todd grinned. He loved making the basketball go exactly where he wanted. Even in a little two-on-two half-court game.

"Air Patman with the ball!" Bruce boasted. He faked left around Aaron Dallas, drove right, and jumped, releasing the ball at the last second. Todd watched it spin through the air. *Go in*, he urged silently, and a second later the ball thunked off the backboard and into the net.

"Air Patman?" Ken yelled as he picked up the ball and passed it to Aaron. "In your dreams."

"I'd have blocked it," Aaron insisted, "except that I twisted my knee last week and it still hurts to jump."

Todd rolled his eyes. "You couldn't have jumped that high anyway," he said.

Aaron curled his lip. "I can jump higher than you any day of the week, Wilkins," he said. "And twice on Sundays."

"Sundaes?" Ken licked his lips. "Did someone say something about ice cream sundaes?"

"Hey, guys, concentrate on the game," Bruce barked, hands on hips. "Let's save the funny stuff for later."

"The bunny stuff?" Ken cupped a hand to his ear and grinned at Todd. "Bunny stuff? You turning into a rabbit or something, Patman?"

Todd snickered. "I can see his big pink ears now," he said.

"No, Patman isn't a rabbit," Ken said, hustling after the ball. "Let's lay off him. He's going to *marry* a rabbit, that's all."

Todd couldn't help laughing. He dribbled toward the basket, looking for an opening.

"Don't laugh!" Bruce said proudly. "I'd rather marry a rabbit than, ugh, a girl." He held up his hands. "C'mon, Wilkins. Hit me with an alley-oop."

"What's wrong with girls?" Aaron wanted to know. He deftly tossed a pass to Ken. "If I had to choose one, I'd take—let me see . . ." His eyes lit up. "J.W."

J.W. Todd frowned. *Jessica Wakefield, of course. And Jessica Wakefield is the twin sister of—*

Suddenly Todd's stomach began to churn.

"Oh, J.W.," Ken said, nodding knowingly. "Sure, she's kind of hot. If you like that sort of thing. But I thought you were nuts for her friend. You know— L.F." He winked.

That's Lila Fowler, Todd thought. *Who was best friends with Jessica Wakefield. Who was still the twin sister of—*

Todd's stomach churned harder.

"L.F.'s pretty cool too," Aaron said with a shrug. "She'd be my second choice."

Ken's eyebrows shot up. "Guess they won't be best friends for long," he commented. Leaning back, he took a shot. The ball clattered off the backboard and bounced into Bruce's hands.

"Girls are boring," Bruce argued. He set up for a three-pointer. "Who cares about dating anyway? I mean, girls just try to change your whole image, that's all. Who needs it?"

Todd watched the ball sail through the hoop. Three more points. "Great shot, Bruce!" he called out.

"Girls are just plain inferior," Bruce went on with a sideways glance at Todd. "Don't you think so, Mr. Teammate?"

Todd hoped he wasn't blushing. He tried hard to look away. The whole topic of girls embarrassed him.

"I don't know," Ken said thoughtfully. "I've always kind of, you know, admired A.S. If you know what I mean."

A.S. That one was easy. Todd stared down at his shoes. Amy Sutton was best friends with—

Bruce handed the ball off to Ken. "Go score one for A.S. If you can." He winked at Todd. "Amy Sutton Matthews. Hey, I can see it! What do you think, Wilkins? Girls are totally inferior, right?"

Todd took a deep breath. Here it was—the moment he'd been dreading. "Well, maybe some girls," he said weakly.

"Huh?" Bruce put his hands on his hips. "*Which* girls? And how about the *other* ones?"

Todd could feel his skin turn red from his toes to the roots of his hair. "Other girls aren't. Inferior, I mean," he added quickly. "Like, um, for instance, E.W." There. He'd said it.

"E.W.?" Ken paused on the way to the basket. "You mean, like, Elizabeth Wakefield? Jessica's sister?"

Todd could barely nod. "She's, um, one of the smartest kids in the school." He had a lot of respect for Elizabeth's mind. Besides the fact that she was just a really cool kid, with lots of personality. And pretty. No doubt about it, Elizabeth was someone he wanted to get to know better.

Someday.

"Oh, give me a break!" Bruce signaled a time-out just as Ken's shot banked into the basket. "Maybe it's too advanced for a little mind such as yours, Wilkins, but there's a humongous difference between getting good grades—like Elizabeth does—and being *smart*. Like me," he added.

Like Bruce? Todd thought in surprise, but he kept his mouth shut.

"I don't care if Elizabeth gets sixty zillion on her math tests," Bruce went on. "She isn't, you know, creative. She just studies hard, is all. That's not the same thing." He shrugged.

Todd bit his lip. Of course Elizabeth was creative. She wrote articles, didn't she? She edited the paper, didn't she? "How well did *you* do on the math test?" he asked.

"Thirty-six," Ken put in before Bruce could speak.

"Thirty-*seven*," Bruce corrected him icily. "But who needs to know fractions, huh? I know other stuff. Important stuff." He sighed impatiently. "And Elizabeth said she probably wouldn't even cover the skateboard petition in the *Sixers*. The kid wouldn't know news if it bit her. The biggest issue of my *life*, and she—" He broke off. "You guys are nuts. Girls are totally inferior, and you heard it here first."

Todd shook his head. Hanging with Patman could make anybody crazy. "I can't agree with that," he said softly.

"So don't agree!" Bruce snorted. "But if Elizabeth's so awesome, how come you guys aren't a real couple, huh? How come you haven't been dating for, like, the last eight years?"

Because we were only four years old eight years ago, Todd thought. But Bruce's comment bugged him. "Well—because—" he began. He licked his lips. "Because—" he tried again.

Quickly Todd reflected back on times when he'd sort of accidentally-on-purpose run into Elizabeth in the hallway. Times when they'd danced at school parties until he got shy and went to stand with Ken and Bruce. Times when he'd written an article for the *Sixers* just so he'd have an excuse to call her on the phone after school. Todd sighed. *As far as I'm concerned, Elizabeth and I are together!*

But he wasn't sure Elizabeth would see it the same way.

"Quit stalling," Bruce said, tapping his foot impatiently. "See, I don't date because I think girls stink. What's your excuse?" He leaned forward and stared directly into Todd's eyes.

Todd took a deep breath. He knew a challenge when he heard one. He only hoped he could rise to it. "I'm, um, you know, planning to ask her out this weekend," he heard himself saying. *Sheesh. Now I've done it.* Todd clamped his mouth shut, but it was too late. The words were out.

Bruce's lips spread into a big smile. He jerked his thumb at Todd. "I'll believe it when I see it," he said.

Two

◇

"What are you doing, Jessica?" Elizabeth asked curiously. Elizabeth had come into the living room after dinner to find her twin staring at some cards she'd spread on the coffee table. There was a purple towel wrapped loosely around Jessica's head.

"Reading the tarot," Jessica said in a mysterious voice. She pronounced it "tare-oh." She waved her hand across the layout in front of her. "This deck of cards contains all the secrets of the universe."

Elizabeth grinned. "Let me see." She set down the folder of hypnosis information that Mr. Bowman had given her. *Tarot cards*, she thought. *Figures*. She didn't know much about tarot cards, but she knew that they had something to do with fortune-telling. She leaned over her sister's shoulder.

"Careful!" Jessica snapped. "You might disturb the psychic vibrations."

Psychic vibrations? Elizabeth forced back a snicker. From a distance the cards looked perfectly normal, but up close she could see they didn't come from a regular deck. There was a king with swords, and a knight of some kind, and something that looked like a cup. "And you think these things can really tell your fortune?" she asked skeptically.

"Of course." With a sudden motion Jessica scooped the deck into her hand. "Here, I'll give you a reading," she offered.

"No, thanks!" Elizabeth shuddered. She tapped the folder. "Listen, I've been reading up on hypnosis, and it's all a fraud. Why should tarot readings be any different?"

"Because," Jessica said, deftly shuffling the cards. "Anyway, who says hypnosis is fake? I don't believe it."

"Lots of people," Elizabeth said. She opened the folder and found a quote from a physics professor at the University of Chicago. "Top scientists."

"Oh, scientists," Jessica said dismissively.

Elizabeth sighed. Arguing with her twin was usually pretty difficult. It was even tougher when Jessica was in her Incredible Madame Jessica mode. "Just let me read you one thing, OK?" Elizabeth asked, sliding onto the couch.

Jessica made a face. "OK. *If* I get to do a reading on you afterward." She held out the cards expectantly.

Elizabeth rolled her eyes, but she nodded. *What harm*

can it do? she asked herself. "'Some stage hypnotists carry containers of itching powder,'" she read aloud. "'At the right moment, they turn away from the audience and open the containers, pretending to sneeze to cover the act of blowing the powder around the stage. Then they tell their subjects to feel as if they're itching all over.'" Elizabeth shut the folder. "Well?"

Jessica shrugged. "First, it only said *'some* stage hypnotists.' It didn't say *'all* stage hypnotists.'" She dealt out the top few cards from the deck. "And second, so what? Maybe it would have worked without itching powder. How do you know it wouldn't?"

Elizabeth frowned. "Because it's stupid, that's why. Because it doesn't make sense."

"Aha," Jessica said in a soft voice. "Who says it has to make sense?"

"Well—" Elizabeth groped for words. "Well, there has to be a reasonable explanation. People don't just start itching because somebody tells them to."

Jessica shrugged. "People do lots of things because other people tell them to. Like, I cleaned my room last week because Mom told me to."

Elizabeth took a deep breath. "That's different. Anyway, you didn't *really* clean your room. You just pushed everything under the bed."

"I only pushed a few things under the bed," Jessica said with dignity. She adjusted her turban so it wouldn't fall off. "And Mom didn't need itching powder to make me clean, did she?"

"No, but—" Elizabeth began, feeling totally

confused. "Are you telling me that Mom *hypnotized* you into cleaning your room?"

"Well, you know how often I clean up my room," Jessica said.

Elizabeth did know. Once every sixty-three years or so. "But—" she began again.

"What other explanation do you have?" Jessica wanted to know. "This is a very mysterious world, with strange forces at work." She pressed one finger to her lips. "You should pay more attention to your horoscope," she said importantly. "Do you know what it said today?"

"No, what did it say today?" Elizabeth asked, pretending to yawn. She never bothered to read the horoscope. And with good reason, she thought.

"Your horoscope," Jessica informed her, "said that you should listen to your relatives."

Elizabeth smiled. "We were born on the same day," she said, "so our horoscopes must be the same. So that means *you* should listen to *me*. And I'm telling you, it's a lot of baloney."

Jessica shook her head. "There are things in this world that even you don't know about," she said in a spooky voice. She held up a slim paperback book. "I bought this secondhand. It's called *Tapping Your Inner Powers*." She looked at Elizabeth warningly. "It's dangerous to laugh at mysterious forces."

Elizabeth felt a sudden chill. *Not because of what Jessica said,* she assured herself. *It's just that I need to put on a sweater. Or something.*

*   *   *

"Let's see," Jessica muttered as she pondered the arrangement of cards in front of her. The King of Wands was upside down, which meant something, although she couldn't remember what, and the Nine of Swords was next to it, and that had to do with math and numbers or the moon or one of those things, and—

She frowned and stared harder, hoping that everything would become clear.

Elizabeth made a face. "How many readings have you done anyway, Jess?"

"Oh, lots," Jessica assured her. *More than zero anyway*, she added to herself. "It's just that, you know, every arrangement of the tarot is different. That's because everybody's life is different," she explained. "The answer to all life's mysteries may lie in the cards."

That was a direct quote from page thirty-nine of *Tapping Your Inner Powers*. Jessica especially liked that line. It was nice to think that the answer to all life's mysteries lay somewhere—and why not in the cards? Jessica just wished they hadn't thrown that little word *may* in there.

Elizabeth's only response was a shake of the head.

"I'm serious!" Jessica exclaimed, staring daggers at her sister. It was always hard to argue with Elizabeth. Especially when Elizabeth was in her everything-has-a-reasonable-explanation mode. "See, your life isn't Lila's or mine or anybody else's. So the cards come out differently for you."

"But you dealt them," Elizabeth pointed out. "You shuffled them and put them out. How does psychic stuff get in there?"

Jessica sighed. "It's too complicated to explain," she said. "It only works in the hands of a true believer." That was another line from *Tapping Your Inner Powers.* "But I'm psychic, Elizabeth, and something happens when I lay the cards out. I feel a tingling in my fingers." *Most of the time anyway.*

"All right." Elizabeth rubbed her eyes. "So what's going to happen in my future?" she asked.

"Well—" Jessica hesitated. Grabbing her book, she opened it to the section on tarot cards and located the Page of Cups—the first card in the layout in front of her.

" 'You are going to get an invitation from a friend or an admirer,' " she read.

"Huh?" Elizabeth made a face.

"Just what I said," Jessica explained. "You're going to get an invitation from—"

"Get real," Elizabeth said, smiling. "What kind of a prediction is that? That happens to everybody sooner or later."

Jessica had to admit that was true. She ran her finger down the rest of the page. "Let's see—the Page of Cups also says that you might become, um, a dancer, or a set designer, or something like that."

Elizabeth scratched her head. "Dancing? Set design? Last time I looked, I had two left feet. And the only A's I ever got in art were for effort. Is that the best you can do?"

"Well, I'm still learning," Jessica defended herself. "Remember, the cards are only a tool, not an end in themselves." She wasn't entirely sure what that meant, but it sounded good. She'd read it on page seventy-two of *Tapping Your Inner Powers*.

"I think they're the wrong kind of tool," Elizabeth remarked. "It's like digging up a sidewalk with a tablespoon."

Jessica ignored her twin. Her eyes moved to the next card. "Here we are!" she said triumphantly. "The Nine of Swords. 'You will be involved with calculations and business contracts. . . .'" Her voice trailed off. *Yeah, right.* "Well—let's see what else the Nine of Swords means. Um—it says you will have stomach problems," she told her sister.

"Stomach problems?" Elizabeth giggled.

"Don't you feel sick?" Jessica asked hopefully.

"Not exactly," Elizabeth said. "But if you keep up ridiculous predictions like this for much longer, I just might."

Jessica decided to ignore her sister. "The Queen of Wands," she said aloud, fingering the next card. "Aha! You should expect to hear some *very* good news," she reported, consulting the book. "You have great power to get the things you want. And get this—you're going to be an actor, an entertainer, or a major player in the fashion world." She winked at Elizabeth. "How about *that*?"

Elizabeth shook her head. "To tell you the truth, that sounds more like you," she remarked.

Jessica frowned. *Actor. Entertainer. Fashion world.* Elizabeth was right. That did sound an awful lot like the future she'd planned for herself. She studied the card more closely. "The card's pointing toward me," she said. "So maybe it isn't going to be your future at all, but mine." It sounded reasonable enough. "And isn't it amazing that the cards picked up on that right away?" she asked happily. "How can you doubt their powers?"

"Amy?"

"Up here, Mom!" Amy Sutton called out. She was sitting on her bed after dinner Tuesday night, trying to decide if she should eat the candy bar she'd saved for dessert or if she should finish her math homework first.

Mrs. Sutton appeared in the doorway. "Can we talk for a few minutes?" she asked.

"Sure." Amy patted the bed beside her, wondering what her mother had in mind.

Mrs. Sutton slid next to her daughter. "We're doing something very interesting at the station," she told Amy, "and I thought you might like to be involved."

"Me?" Amy's heart gave a leap. Her mother, a television reporter, often appeared on camera for one of the local stations. "How?" *Maybe I'll get to be interviewed,* she thought. She could see herself up on the screen already. . . .

Mrs. Sutton smiled. "We're doing a feature on women who are pilots," she explained.

"On pilots?" Amy frowned. She didn't see what that had to do with her. She was too young to be a pilot, and she didn't exactly like flying. In fact, the idea of flying terrified her.

"There are a lot of women pilots nowadays," Mrs. Sutton went on, "and we're interested in finding out how their jobs affect their daughters."

Their daughters? "But Mom," Amy said, "you're not a pilot, so how can I—"

Mrs. Sutton laughed. "Of course I'm not a pilot. And we're not interested in interviewing you."

"Oh." Amy picked up the candy bar. She couldn't imagine why her mother wanted her, then. Maybe she just wanted to see if Amy knew any kids whose mothers were pilots. She wrinkled her nose. That wouldn't be as much fun as being on camera.

"But a lot of these daughters will be about your age or younger," Mrs. Sutton said, settling back against Amy's pillow. "The other reporters and I don't talk to kids as well as we might, and we thought it would be interesting to get questions from someone closer to their age." She winked at Amy. "So how about it? Interested in interviewing these girls? On camera?"

Amy's head whirled. "Am I *interested?*" She flung herself forward and off the bed with a whoop. "You *bet* I'm interested!" Interviewing other kids on camera! It sounded way better than interviewing kids around school for the *Sixers*. She could see herself, a fancy new hairstyle in place, signing off after the broadcast. . . .

"This special report has been brought to you by the Suttons," she'd say. *"This is Amy Sutton. Now back to you in the studio, Mike."*

Mrs. Sutton smiled. "I take it you're interested."

"Just wait till I tell Elizabeth!" Amy shouted. She was so excited, she could barely get the words out. "When do we start?"

"Next week sometime," her mother said, "but we haven't set a date. The first interview will be with the woman who pilots the traffic helicopter for one of the radio stations. She's got a seven-year-old daughter, who'll be coming up with us too. So I'll talk to the mom while you get to know the daughter and ask her a few questions."

Coming up with us? Amy's throat constricted. Suddenly she couldn't breathe. "I have to go *up* in one of those things?"

"What's wrong?" Mrs. Sutton's eyes filled with concern.

I'm terrified of flying! Amy wanted to shout. But she didn't.

"Amy?" Mrs. Sutton touched her shoulder.

"Couldn't we—you know—do the interview on the ground?" Amy begged. She laughed nervously, hoping she didn't sound like a coward. "There'd be more room. And it wouldn't be as noisy."

"On the ground?" Her mother frowned. "I don't think so, sweetheart. Journalistically speaking, it wouldn't have the same zing."

Amy nodded slowly. Her mother was right, she

knew. It made sense to give the viewer a you-are-there feeling.

But she didn't *like* flying. The sky was too high up, that was all there was to it. You sat in a tiny metal box with wings, and when the wind blew or it rained, you got pushed around, and there were mountains and tall buildings to crash into. Her stomach hurt. *And what if the propeller stops whirling or the engine stops running?* she asked herself. *I'd sink like a stone, down and down and—*

Her stomach hurt even more.

"Don't you want to do this?" Mrs. Sutton asked, peering closely into Amy's eyes. "Because if you don't, we—"

"I *do* want to do it," Amy protested. And she did. *This is my big chance,* she told herself, but the idea didn't make her feel any braver. She flashed her mother a weak smile. "No problem. And, um, thanks for asking me."

"You're very welcome," her mother said. "I know you'll do a great job."

Amy nodded.

She *would* do a great job, she told herself when her mother left the room.

If she could get into the stupid helicopter to begin with.

Amy bit her lip so hard she could almost taste blood.

She'd have to find a way to get over her fear.

Somehow.

Three

"Keep it down to a dull roar, please, class," Mr. Bowman said in homeroom the next morning. "I have an announcement to make about tomorrow's assembly."

Todd stared straight ahead, at Elizabeth Wakefield, who was three rows in front of him. He spent most of his homeroom time just watching her. He felt as though he knew everything about her: the way she held her pencil, how she'd divided her notebook into six sections with different-colored loose-leaf paper in each section, the way she'd twitch her shoulders when she was about to raise her hand . . .

Todd sighed. *But what does she know about me?* he wondered. *Probably nothing.* He'd have to find a way to talk to her if he really was going to ask her out that weekend. The whole idea made him sweat all over.

"We're privileged to have a very special guest," Mr. Bowman went on. "Her name is Dr. Q, and she's a hypnotist."

"A hypnotist?" Jessica Wakefield bounced out of her seat. "Awesome!"

"Some people believe that hypnosis is a fake," Mr. Bowman went on. "Others say it really does exist. Many people use it to calm their fears."

Fears? Todd sat bolt upright.

"Hey, man!" Bruce whispered excitedly. "There's your answer. Just get the doc to hypnotize you, that's all, and you'll be able to ask ol' Wakefield out." He dissolved into a fit of laughter.

Todd rolled his eyes. It wasn't a joke. He focused on Elizabeth, and he felt his heart thudding in his chest the way it did whenever he thought about her. Maybe Dr. Q really *could* hypnotize him into not being afraid of her.

"Mr. Bowman?" Jessica raised her hand. "How will Dr. Q choose volunteers?"

Todd leaned forward, wanting to hear the answer too.

"Good question, Jessica," Mr. Bowman said thoughtfully, adjusting his tie. "I'm not really sure. Are you interested in being chosen?"

Jessica's head bobbed up and down. "I'm learning about the spirit world in my spare time," she announced. "I already can do tarot readings and I can sort of tell the future, and I think hypnosis would be totally cool."

Todd was barely listening. He was still watching Elizabeth. She had a faint grin on her face. Then her shoulders twitched, and her hand shot up.

"I think hypnosis is a total fraud," she said. "When Dr. Q comes, we should all be careful not to be fooled."

"My sister is completely wrong," Jessica interrupted. "Hypnosis is wonderful. We should all pay attention to its powers. Hypnosis gives you strength you don't know you have."

"Really?" Amy Sutton leaned forward.

"No way," Elizabeth sighed, rolling her eyes. "That's just what they want you to believe."

Todd was torn. Part of him wished that hypnotism would work on him and make it easier for him to approach Elizabeth. But part of him wanted Elizabeth to be right, because—well, because she was Elizabeth. Todd flipped open his notebook and started doodling.

"But hypnotists really do things that can't be explained!" Ellen Riteman was speaking now. "I saw one show where the guy took this piece of paper and wrote a note on it, and he didn't let anyone see it, and then—"

A note. Todd's pulse quickened. Maybe he could write a note and slip it into Elizabeth's locker. Checking to make sure no one was watching, he turned to a blank page in his notebook and started to write.

He only hoped he would have the courage to sign it.

*   *   *

Sighing loudly, Elizabeth dialed her locker combination. It was lunchtime, but she was still thinking about the discussion in homeroom that morning.

She couldn't figure out how so many kids could be fooled like that. Annoyed, Elizabeth twirled the dial left to thirty-eight and right again to sixteen. "They'd probably believe in killer robins," she muttered aloud. "And sharks that fly."

Speaking of killers . . . she could already see herself sitting in Dr. Q's office, doing her killer interview. She couldn't wait to sink her teeth into the "doctor." *"Dr. Q," I'll say in a no-nonsense tone of voice, "let's be completely honest with each other. There's no such thing as hypnosis, right?" Then I'll cross my arms and stare at her. And Dr. Q will shake her head and admit that she's a fake.* Elizabeth nodded. *Dr. Q will beg me to keep her secret, but as a journalist, I won't be able to do that, of course.*

Elizabeth pointed the dial to two and yanked open the locker. To her surprise, a sheet of paper floated to the floor.

What's this? Frowning, Elizabeth stooped to pick it up. It wasn't her own loose-leaf paper, that was for sure. The sheet had been folded three times, and "Elizabeth Wakefield" was printed across the outside in small block letters. *Someone must have stuck a note into my locker,* Elizabeth realized, running her finger lightly along the edge of the paper. The writing didn't look familiar—and yet . . .

Wait a minute.

Her heart gave a thump.

Todd Wilkins has paper just like this, she thought. She remembered the time a few weeks before when she'd kind of casually asked to borrow some paper from him in homeroom, even though Amy was closer. Even though lots of people were closer. Elizabeth's mouth felt dry. Maybe the note was from Todd.

But it couldn't be. Todd barely knew she existed, right? Leaning against the row of lockers, she opened the paper, almost afraid of what she'd find.

She decided to begin reading at the top and work her way slowly down, saving the signature for the very end. Just in case.

"8:45 Wed., homeroom

Dear Elizabeth,

Hi. This discussion is kind of boring. Don't you think so?

Well, I was just wondering if you wanted to go to a movie. With me, I mean. Saturday night. We could go see the Eileen Thomas movie if you wanted. Or if you didn't want to, we could do something else. Like I don't know what, but maybe we could think of something.

My dad and me can pick you up.

But if you're really busy I understand.

Yours,
Todd

P.S.: Wilkins, that is"

*   *   *

Elizabeth let her hand fall to her side, with the letter in it.

Yes!

Her heart sang. Todd Wilkins had invited her on a date! A real live date! To a real live movie! An Eileen Thomas movie, where the characters had actual conversations, not some shoot-'em-up Arnold Weissenhammer film like Bruce Patman would go to.

Elizabeth felt warm all over. Shoving her books into her locker, she skipped off toward the cafeteria, her feet scarcely touching the ground.

Todd Wilkins likes me! she thought. *He really likes me!*

"I'm telling you guys," Bruce said, shaking his head. "This Dr. Q is a total lunatic." He twisted his spaghetti into a huge ball around his fork. "Anybody who thinks she can hypnotize *me*—"

"He's right, Wilkins," Ken agreed. Todd, Ken, and Bruce were eating lunch in the cafeteria. "I mean, I hate to say it, but I just don't think this hypnosis stuff makes sense."

"See?" Bruce said. "Even Matthews agrees with me. Good man, Matthews." He patted Ken on the back.

"You're just conceited," Todd said. "You simply don't want to admit that someone could have power over you, is all."

Bruce took a long drink of water. "No one's getting power over the great Patman. Especially not some *female*. Some inferior being." He spoke the words with great disgust.

Todd couldn't help laughing. "I don't know," he said. "It just seems to me that maybe there's something in hypnosis. Remember what Mr. Bowman was saying about fears. Some people overcome their fears when they get hypnotized." *Like me, I hope.* "For instance."

"And you believed it?" Bruce stared sorrowfully at Todd. "Who needs to overcome their fears anyway?" he demanded. "Just don't be afraid. Act brave, even if you're a wimp, and everything will be OK." He nudged Ken in the ribs. "Right, Matthews?"

"Um—right," Ken agreed hesitantly.

"Take this skateboarding-in-the-halls stuff, for instance," Bruce continued grandly. He rested his elbows on the table and scooped lime Jell-O into his mouth. "I mean, if you turn tail every time you want something, you never get anywhere. Now, me, I'm no wimp, and I sure didn't need hypnosis to go see Mr. Clark about skateboarding."

"Which he said no about," Todd reminded him.

"Details," Bruce assured him. "So I started a petition instead. Hypnosis! It's for losers!"

Todd sighed. He wanted to argue with Bruce. But if he did, sooner or later Bruce would demand to know why he wanted to believe in hypnosis. Which would mean that he'd have to tell Bruce about wanting to feel less shy about Elizabeth.

He nodded. "Well, maybe you're right, Patman."

"*Maybe* I'm right?" Bruce snorted. "I'm *always* right."

Todd turned his thoughts to Elizabeth. He wondered if she was coming to the cafeteria that day. He wondered if she'd gotten his note. What if she'd thrown it out without reading it? What if she'd laughed at the idea of going on a date with him? Maybe she was showing it to all her friends right at that moment. Maybe she was posting it in the girls' bathroom with a comment that said, "Get a load of this!" Maybe—

There was a light tap on his shoulder.

"Huh?" Todd burst out, spinning around and nearly upsetting his glass of chocolate milk. His heart began to race. And when he saw who was behind him, it beat even faster.

"Hello, Todd," Elizabeth said.

Todd stared. "Um—hi," he said weakly, barely able to squeeze the words through his suddenly dry lips.

He cleared his throat. Elizabeth was smiling, which was a good sign—unless it was a mocking smile? "I mean, hi," he said, dropping his voice an octave. "Um, how are you?"

"Fine, thanks." Elizabeth kept smiling.

Bruce leaned forward, his eyebrows raised, but Todd ignored him. He held his breath, hoping he'd remembered to sign his name on the note after all. "Um, what's up?" he asked, hoping he sounded kind of casual and not totally terrified.

"The answer is yes," Elizabeth said simply. And she turned and walked away.

Yes! Todd exhaled. He would have pumped his fist, but he felt too weak. *Yes!* He stared at Elizabeth as she disappeared, committing to memory everything about her all over again.

" 'Yes'?" Ken leaned over and folded his arms. "Did I hear that right? Elizabeth Wakefield said yes?"

"Va-va-voom!" Bruce said. "Of course, she was probably just saying, 'Yes, you can borrow my notes since I'm so smart.' "

"Maybe we could call Todd Lover Boy," Ken suggested. "Or better yet, we can carve their initials all over the school. You know, T.W. and E.W., in a heart with an arrow through it."

Todd rolled his eyes. They could tease him all day for all he cared.

Yes! he thought again, this time thrusting a fist triumphantly in the air. *She said yes!*

Then he frowned.

She did mean yes, she'd go out with me, right?

Four

◇

"This is going to be *so* cool," Lila said.

Jessica nodded in agreement. It was Thursday at last—the day of the big assembly.

"I'll be so bummed if I'm not picked to be one of her volunteers," Lila went on.

"I'm pretty sure I'll be picked," Jessica said. *I'd better!* she thought. *How will I learn about hypnosis if I don't participate in the show?* "There's this little voice in my head saying she'll choose me. I'm kind of psychic, you know."

At least, if she shut her eyes and listened hard, she could almost hear a voice saying that.

"Oh, really?" Lila asked. "I'm psychic too."

Yeah, sure you're psychic, Jessica thought, annoyed. Why did Lila always have to horn in on whatever Jessica was doing? "Just because I'm psychic doesn't mean you have to be psychic," she said aloud.

"I *am* psychic," Lila replied. "I've *always* been psychic. Ever since I was, like, two."

"You have not either," Jessica said, rolling her eyes.

"But what I really want is to meet her afterward," Lila said. Her eyes sparkled. "That would be *totally* cool."

Meet her? "I sure hope we can," Jessica said casually, as if she'd had the idea for weeks. "I've been wanting to pick Dr. Q's brain, since I'm planning to learn how to do hypnosis."

The previous night hadn't gone well in the psychic department, Jessica had to admit. *Tapping Your Inner Powers* wasn't as helpful as she'd expected. It seemed as though every tarot card had thirty possible interpretations. More than once Jessica had been utterly muddled trying to predict her own future.

Worse yet, the card that had kept coming up the previous night was the Queen of Swords. According to the book, that card meant that Jessica was unreliable, narrow-minded, and a gossip. (Ha!) It also meant that she'd become a computer programmer, a scientist, or a secretary. Nothing about fashion, drama, money, or anything even remotely *good*. After seeing the Queen of Swords staring up at her for about the fifth time, Jessica had decided that maybe the tarot wasn't all it was cracked up to be.

But hypnosis made sense. Jessica leaned closer

to Lila. "You can be my first subject when I'm an expert," she promised. *Which won't be long, if I have anything to say about it!*

"Did you read the last issue of the *National Braggart*, Jessica?" Lila frowned. "About how Johnny Buck is really an alien? They talked to, like, one of his doctors, who said they found some strange metal in his head when they did an X ray. Do you think Dr. Q would know about that?"

Jessica felt a surge of irritation. *Honestly*, she thought, *some people will believe anything!* She tried to make her voice cheerful. "Why would a hypnotist care about something like that, Lila? And Johnny Buck isn't an alien. I think we'd know."

"Oh." Lila wrinkled her nose. "But—"

"Shhh!" Jessica put her fingers to her lips. The lights had suddenly dimmed. "I think it's about to start!" She leaned forward and rubbed her palms together in anticipation. No matter what anybody said, she had psychic gifts. She knew she did.

And Dr. Q was the person to help her develop them.

"For my demonstration, I'd like several volunteers," Dr. Q said a few minutes later. She stood on the stage, her arms outstretched, as if inviting kids to come up.

Amy licked her lips nervously. Ignoring Elizabeth's look of disapproval, she shot her hand into the air. *Maybe it's all baloney*, she thought. *But if I can stop being scared of helicopters, then it's worth trying, right?*

Amy had been disappointed when Dr. Q had come onstage. The doctor hadn't looked mysterious at all. There was a purple robe draped around her shoulders, sure, and Dr. Q was a tall woman with piercing blue eyes that seemed to stare right through you. But there was no pointy hat, no movie theme music, no weird hairstyles or foreign accent.

"Amy!" Elizabeth hissed. "Put your hand down!"

Amy inched away from her friend. She would put her hand in the air if she wanted. Every time she thought of that helicopter ride, she practically passed out. But she was going to do that interview. In the air.

Somehow.

Whether Elizabeth liked it or not!

She's not going to pick me, Jessica thought frantically. There were only six chairs on the stage, and four were already full. So far Dr. Q had ignored her waving hand. Instead, she'd picked Bruce Patman—*Bruce Patman, for crying out loud!*—and three kids Jessica didn't know very well. Jessica concentrated on sending thought waves to Dr. Q. *Pick me—me—*

Dr. Q's gaze swept through the audience. Jessica held her breath as those piercing eyes flicked toward her—and then sighed in despair as they passed her by.

Only two empty chairs!

Desperate times called for desperate measures. Quickly Jessica vaulted out of her seat and dashed for the stage. "Thanks for picking me!" she shouted. She'd just have to pretend she'd misunderstood— and hope that Dr. Q didn't have the heart to get rid of her. The lights on the stage were much brighter than the lights in the audience. Jessica blinked and headed toward the nearest chair as if she belonged.

Dr. Q frowned. "Weren't you just sitting on the other side of the auditorium?"

Jessica shook her head. "That's my twin sister," she said dismissively. "You wouldn't want *her* as a subject, Dr. Q. She doesn't even believe in hypnosis." She sighed and made a face, showing Dr. Q that she herself, on the other hand, would make an excellent subject.

"Ah." Dr. Q's long arm swept out toward Elizabeth. "Twins," she said in a deep voice. "I like working with twins. Especially when one is a believer and the other a skeptic."

Jessica felt a jolt of energy rush through her body. There was a tingly feeling in her palms.

Now Elizabeth would see the truth. She'd see how an expert did things. She'd see proof that hypnosis was real.

Another jolt shot through Jessica. She couldn't believe Elizabeth didn't feel that energy too.

No matter what her sister might *say* . . .

Elizabeth blinked in the light as she arrived on the stage. She hadn't exactly wanted to be up there, but in the time it had taken her to mount the steps, she had changed her mind.

This will be a great opportunity to see how Dr. Q cheats, she told herself. She'd pretend to be hypnotized along with the others. But instead of going under, she'd be watching. She'd have Dr. Q under constant surveillance. The hypnotist wouldn't be able to make a move without Elizabeth's taking it all in.

She grinned to herself. *And the next issue of the* Sixers *will have an exposé on the tricks Dr. Q used to fool us. Most of us anyway. Written by yours truly, the youngest investigative reporter west of the Mississippi!*

"So you are a nonbeliever." Dr. Q motioned Elizabeth toward the last empty chair.

Despite herself, Elizabeth started at Dr. Q's words. She sat down, her heart beating rapidly. *It's just a costume,* she told herself, trying to imagine Dr. Q out of the robe and in a pair of jogging shorts instead. And the color of those strangely unsettling blue eyes probably just came from contact lenses, Elizabeth decided. "Well, I have a few questions," she replied, trying not to sound like the total nonbeliever she was.

Dr. Q nodded solemnly. "Very well," she said. "Perhaps you will find that today's demonstration answers some of them."

Elizabeth strained to catch a glimpse inside Dr. Q's billowy sleeve without being too obvious. "Probably," she said, wondering how Jessica could fall for this stuff.

Deep down, she couldn't believe that Jessica could be quite so gullible, despite whatever her sister might *say*. . . .

Dr. Q reached into the pocket of her robe faster

than Elizabeth could follow with her eyes. A split
second later a golden pocket watch was in her
hand. Dr. Q turned the watch this way and that,
catching the reflection of the auditorium lights on
the shiny polished surface.

"I will now tell my subjects to keep their eyes on
the watch," Dr. Q announced. "Relax every muscle,
please. Begin with your toes and work your way
up your body to your brain."

To your brain? Elizabeth tried hard not to laugh.

"I sense negative vibrations," Dr. Q continued,
not looking at Elizabeth. Slowly at first, then faster
and faster, she swung the watch back and forth.
"The brain must be relaxed too. Hypnosis requires
a calm, untroubled mind." The watch swung in
wider arcs from Dr. Q's hand.

The room was absolutely silent. Elizabeth's eyes
were drawn toward the moving golden watch. Dr.
Q's hand barely twitched, yet somehow the watch
maintained its speed. Elizabeth furrowed her brow,
wondering how she did it.

Slowly, gently, Dr. Q raised her free arm.
"Imagine that you are riding an elevator," she said
softly. Elizabeth noticed that she timed her words
to fit the rhythm of the swinging pendulum. "You
are on the top floor of the building. Press the button marked B—for basement."

Next to Elizabeth, Jessica hunched forward. Her
eyes stared intently at the golden watch. "B—for
basement," Jessica repeated. Blindly she stabbed

out a forefinger and hit an imaginary button in front of her. After a moment's hesitation Elizabeth did the same. If she was going to learn Dr. Q's tricks, she'd have to play along.

Quickly she sneaked a glance at her twin. Jessica did look a little glassy-eyed. But of course this wasn't real, she reminded herself. It was just Jessica being Jessica, she decided.

There was silence again. It seemed as though the room was getting darker. Either that, or the watch was growing brighter. Elizabeth bit her lip, watching the movement of the pendulum.

Of course! There's a battery in it, she thought. That made sense. A battery in the watch that made it glow and kept it moving. She longed to get her hands on the watch and expose it for the fake that it was.

"You can feel yourself descending in the elevator," Dr. Q said. "Down, further and further. It's a smooth and easy ride. As the elevator moves, leave behind your worries, your fears, your anxieties. Feel the elevator move through the building toward B for basement, always down, ever down."

Dr. Q's voice actually sounded soothing, Elizabeth had to admit. She could almost imagine herself in the elevator. *The woman's a trained actress, that's all,* she reasoned as she started doing multiplication tables in her head. *Two times one is two. Two times two is four. Two times B, I mean three—*

She swallowed hard. No way was she about to fall under the spell.

Dr. Q was speaking again. "With a thump so gentle you can scarcely feel it, the elevator reaches the basement. Your worries are gone." She slid the watch gracefully back into her pocket.

"My worries are gone," Jessica repeated under her breath.

Dr. Q turned to face the audience. "These six subjects are under my influence now," she said. "They are receptive to suggestion, as you will see in the next few moments. No harm will come to them. In the end, I will bring them back to consciousness by taking them mentally up the same elevator in which they just descended."

Yeah, right, Elizabeth thought. She stirred in her seat, looking for signs of trickery. What else was in Dr. Q's pocket? Come to think of it, why did she have pockets at all if not to help her fool people? She could wear her watch around her neck, couldn't she? Or—

"You." Dr. Q pointed at Bruce Patman. "Imagine yourself doing something totally out of character."

"You mean, like, studying?" a voice from the audience piped up. Several kids giggled, but there were quick shushing noises from the seats.

Elizabeth frowned. Bruce was sitting still, not goofing off, which surprised her. During homeroom the day before, he'd argued that hypnosis wasn't real. Elizabeth's frown deepened. Why wasn't Bruce making a big joke out of this?

Dr. Q pointed back to Bruce. "If you are obeying my command, please bark like a dog," she instructed him.

Elizabeth curled her lip. *Bark like a dog. Good grief.*
Instantly Bruce lifted his head and barked three
times. The audience erupted in laughter. Elizabeth
shook her head. But she felt a little uncomfortable.

It's a pretty decent bark, she thought uneasily.

And it was weird how Bruce hadn't seemed to
notice the other kids. Normally he'd have done
silly things to get even more laughs. But Bruce
wasn't moving. Like Jessica, he had a glassy look
on his face, and his breathing was slow and even.

It looked almost as if he really *were* under a
spell.

It can't be, Elizabeth assured herself. No way was
Bruce truly hypnotized. She was sure about that.

Ninety-nine percent sure anyway.

"Ah, the twins," Dr. Q purred a few minutes
later, turning to face Jessica and Elizabeth.

Elizabeth licked her lips. She was beginning to
feel frustrated. So far she hadn't caught Dr. Q
doing anything suspicious at all. Of course, that
didn't mean she wasn't faking it somehow.

Still, it was kind of strange the way Bruce and
the other kids had done exactly what she'd told
them to do.

"The twins," Dr. Q repeated, fixing Elizabeth
with a piercing stare. Elizabeth tried to make her
eyes dull and lifeless, like Jessica's. "One who be-
lieves—and one who does not."

Dr. Q's hand reached toward her pocket but

stopped. "This is only a hypnosis demonstration," she said slowly. "Yet I must warn these twins that I see strange things in their future. Things that neither girl expects."

There's nothing to worry about, Elizabeth told herself, but she could feel her heart pounding despite herself. *It's probably just like those tarot cards Tuesday night.* "An invitation from an admirer," she repeated under her breath. That was what Jessica had predicted for her, and people were *always* getting invitations from admirers, weren't they? And besides—

Wait a minute.

Nervously Elizabeth chewed her lower lip. It *was* kind of peculiar how Todd's note had come the very next day. Almost as if the cards had known he would write one.

But that was impossible, of course.

"Listen well," the hypnotist said in a low voice that seemed to rumble across the stage. "Neither of you respects the dangers of the unknown." She lifted an arm and pointed accusingly at Jessica, then Elizabeth. "The forces of the universe cannot be controlled," she said. "But they are there all the same."

"They are there," Jessica repeated. She sat with her head back, her eyes completely closed. "They are there."

"But that is not why we are here today," Dr. Q said in a more normal tone of voice. "We have come to see hypnosis at work. I will now tell these two young ladies to switch identities temporarily." She looked sharply at Elizabeth. "When I snap my fingers, you will resume your normal selves. Begin."

"You know, I really don't believe in hypnosis much," Jessica exclaimed, sitting forward. "I mean, it's baloney, don't you think?"

Elizabeth wasn't sure what to do. Should she imitate her sister? *Could* she? Half of her wanted to stand up right there and then and announce that she was only faking. But on the other hand, if there was still more of the demonstration, she'd need to be on the stage to catch Dr. Q in the act. And if she got up now, she'd have to go back to the audience. "Oh, I completely disagree!" she said, trying to sound exactly like her sister. *No. Jessica wouldn't say "completely."* "Hypnosis is, like, totally cool." *There. That was better.*

"You *would* think so," Jessica snapped. She turned to Dr. Q. "Ever since we were little kids, she's gone on and on about being psychic and being in touch with spirits and stuff like that. It drives me crazy."

Elizabeth hastened to think. *Jessica would respond to that pretty angrily,* she decided. "Oh, give me a break!" she said, rolling her eyes in what she hoped was a very Jessica fashion. "Auras, horoscopes, fashion, parties—what else *is* there?"

"The spirit world doesn't exist. There's a reasonable explanation for everything," Jessica intoned.

Elizabeth stole a quick look at her sister. Even now, Jessica looked totally spaced. And in a weird kind of way, the voice that was coming from her didn't sound precisely like her sister's. She gulped.

It sounded like her own.

Elizabeth blinked rapidly. "Would you please get a *life?*" she demanded. It didn't have much to do with the conversation, but it was the sort of thing Jessica liked to say.

"Well, I'll see you later," Jessica said cheerfully. "I have to go feed the poor and homeless."

"Yeah, right," Elizabeth snapped. Who did Jessica think she was, making fun of her like that? To her embarrassment she heard laughter from the audience. "If you would only once in a while—" she began. *No—Jessica would phrase it differently.* "I mean, if you'd, like, for once—"

Dr. Q stepped forward. "I think we have heard enough for now," she said, and snapped her fingers.

Phew. Elizabeth breathed a sigh of relief. It wasn't easy being Jessica.

"It isn't easy being Elizabeth," Jessica murmured from the chair next to Elizabeth's own.

Elizabeth bit her lip and tried not to stare at her sister.

But inside, her heart was beating furiously.

Because—somehow—the voice sounded like her sister's regular voice again. . . .

Five

◇

"I'm so bummed that we couldn't talk to Dr. Q after the show," Lila remarked wistfully, twirling a lock of her hair.

"I know what you mean," Jessica agreed. She'd eaten dinner at the Fowler mansion that night, and the two girls were lounging in Lila's bedroom. "But *I* actually got hypnotized," she said proudly. "Imagine! Me, Jessica Wakefield, getting hypnotized!"

"You were so amazingly lucky," Lila said, wrinkling her nose.

Jessica sat up straight and shoved one of Lila's pillows out of the way. She suddenly had a brilliant idea. "Hey!" she said, trying not to sound too excited. "Listen, Lila. Why don't I hypnotize you? Like, right now?"

"You?" Lila stared wide-eyed at Jessica. "But you don't know how to—"

"Sure I do," Jessica said quickly before Lila could finish her sentence. "It's easy. Once it's done to you, you can do it to anybody else," she assured her friend. "It's like, um, setting a watch or something like that. Once someone shows you how to set a watch, you can teach somebody else."

Lila's stare turned into a frown. "Really?"

Jessica put her hands on her hips. "Lila," she said in a sorrowful voice, "would I lie to you?"

And don't answer that question! she added quickly to herself.

"Watch the pendant," Jessica chanted as she waved Lila's lucky half-dollar in front of her friend's eyes. "Watch . . . the . . . coin." She tried to make her voice as deep and sonorous as Dr. Q's.

"You're swinging it too fast," Lila objected.

"No way!" Jessica said. "Dr. Q waved it exactly this fast. I remember."

"Oh, like you had a radar gun?" Lila asked sarcastically.

Jessica was tempted to throw the coin onto the bed and go home, but where would she get another guinea pig? Not Elizabeth, that was for sure. "All right," she agreed grumpily, slowing the coin down a tiny bit. "How's this?"

"Better," Lila agreed.

"Watch . . . the . . . coin," Jessica repeated in a

voice scarcely above a whisper. She liked the way the coin swung back and forth in her hand with only a gentle flick of the wrist. As if the coin had a mind of its own. "You must relax. Relax every muscle in your body, starting now."

"That isn't the way Dr. Q told you to do it," Lila remarked. "Dr. Q said—"

Jessica felt her body stiffen. "I don't have to do it exactly the same way as Dr. Q," she pointed out icily. "I'm doing it my own way. Now leave me alone. Watch . . . the . . . coin."

Lila leaned back. Her eyes took on a glazed look.

Jessica raised her eyebrows. This was working faster than she'd expected. "Can you hear me?" she asked. "If you can, raise your right arm."

Almost instantly Lila raised her right arm. She murmured something under her breath. Jessica didn't quite catch it, but she thought it sounded like "Yes, master."

Hmmm, Jessica thought. This had possibilities. "Lower your arm," Jessica suggested.

Like a rock, Lila's arm crashed back onto the bed.

Time for the elevator, Jessica thought. But no, she wanted to put her own stamp on it—not just copy what Dr. Q had done. She put down the coin and faced Lila. "You are in a coal mine," she said. "You, um, have to go down to the bottom to get something. To get a shovel."

"A shovel," Lila repeated. She was sitting motionless, her eyes fixed on a point past Jessica's head.

"Reach out and touch the shovel," Jessica said.

"It is right here in front of me," Lila replied tonelessly. "It is big and brown. It has a handle." Her left arm groped into space. "Ow," she said in the same monotone. "I just hit it."

Jessica frowned. This sounded too good to be true. "How come you hit it?" she demanded.

Lila didn't blink. "Because it is dark. Inside a coal mine."

That made sense. Jessica considered. What should she make Lila do? Something embarrassing, probably. "You are in my power," she hissed, wishing she had a few candles to make for a better atmosphere. "At the count of three you will go over to the telephone."

"The telephone," Lila repeated.

"Right, the telephone," Jessica repeated. "And you will call, um, let me see—" Some boy. Not Bruce Patman, of course, and certainly not Aaron Dallas. Maybe Ken Matthews? Or—

Todd. Of course. Boring old Todd Wilkins.

Jessica's eyes lit up. This would be fun. "You'll call Todd Wilkins," she announced, picturing the scene in her mind, "and you will say that you are passionately in love with him and—"

"I will not either!"

Jessica blinked. Lila was standing up from the bed, looking angry. "I'm not going to do *that*," she said, folding her arms.

Jessica wrinkled her nose. "You weren't really hypnotized," she accused Lila.

"Sure I was." Lila spoke scornfully. "You just woke me up out of my trance, that's all, because it was such a stupid suggestion." She made a face. "Todd Wilkins, yuck."

"Don't *lie*," Jessica said meaningfully. "You were never hypnotized to begin with. You're just trying to make me think you're more psychic than me." She glared at her so-called friend.

"I *am* more psychic than you and you know it," Lila insisted, glaring back. "You're just mad because you can't hypnotize me as well as Dr. Q hypnotized you."

"What's going on, girls?" Lila's father appeared at the doorway.

"Oh, nothing, Daddy," Lila said, shrugging. "Jessica's just trying to prove that she's totally psychic and—"

"I'm hypnotizing your daughter," Jessica interrupted quickly. "Only she's not a very good guinea pig."

"Hypnotizing her?" Mr. Fowler raised his eyebrows and smiled at Jessica. "I didn't know you could hypnotize people."

"I'm working at it," Jessica said, ignoring Lila's snort.

"Hmmm." Mr. Fowler stroked his chin. "You know, I don't think I've ever been hypnotized myself. Isn't that interesting?" He ambled into the room and settled himself in one of Lila's chairs. "Any interest in trying to put me under?" he asked hopefully.

Lila made a face. "Give me a break!"

Jessica grinned and gave Lila a swift kick in the shins. "Sure, Mr. Fowler!" she agreed, reaching for Lila's half-dollar.

"Mmm!" Amy's eyes sparkled as she bit into her slice of chocolate fudge layer cake that evening. She smiled across the kitchen table at her mother. "Did you bake this yourself, Mom?"

"I *wish*," Mrs. Sutton said wryly. She popped a forkful into her mouth and smacked her lips. "No, I bought it at the bakery. When in doubt, call a professional—that's my motto."

Amy giggled. She licked a smidgen of frosting off her finger. "I wish I could bake like this."

"Me too," Mrs. Sutton agreed. "I'd love to work at a bakery. Think of the smells!" She closed her eyes and took a deep breath. "Of course, bakers have to get up at three in the morning."

"Ugh." Amy shuddered. She dug back into the cake with her fork. The frosting was especially good.

"And I've never been much of a cook anyway," Mrs. Sutton went on, laughing. "And I have a good job with a television station. And—oh! Speaking of the station, Amy—"

Amy paused with her fork halfway to her mouth. Her stomach did a flip-flop. "What?" she asked, picturing a bouncing, jerking helicopter in her mind.

"The helicopter ride," Mrs. Sutton said, hitting herself gently in the side of the head. "As you kids would say, duh! We've got a date now—a week from Sunday, two in the afternoon."

"A week from Sunday?" Amy set her fork to the side of her plate. The butterflies in her stomach were growing into mice. Little mice, scampering around. She took a deep breath. "Um—in the air?"

"Of course," Mrs. Sutton replied breezily. "As I told you, it'll be tight in the cockpit, but we've got a go-ahead. And the daughter is anxious to meet you," she added, smiling at Amy.

"Oh." Amy looked down at her cake. Once again she'd lost her appetite. "Um—that's nice."

Her mother frowned. "Don't you want to do it, honey?"

Amy took another deep breath and pushed her plate away, wondering how to answer the question.

Tell her you can't do it, a little voice inside her head urged her.

No way! another voice argued. *This is your chance, Amy. Your big chance—don't mess it up!*

"Amy?" Mrs. Sutton asked.

The image of Dr. Q popped suddenly into Amy's mind. Dr. Q, the hypnotist, who had told the kids onstage that day to leave their worries and their anxieties behind. Mr. Bowman had said that hypnotists could help people overcome their fears. Amy set her jaw. She'd waved her hand frantically during the assembly, but Dr. Q hadn't noticed her.

Well, by golly, she'd *make* Dr. Q notice her.

And what better way to do it than through her

best friend, who was planning to do an interview with Dr. Q herself?

"Of course I'll do it, Mom," she promised.

"You are in the middle of a long, dark tunnel," Jessica said in her most mysterious voice.

"In a tunnel," Mr. Fowler repeated. His eyes were shut, and his body was perfectly motionless.

Jessica nodded to herself. This was going well. "See?" she hissed to Lila. "I can too do it."

Lila rolled her eyes.

"And there is a light at the end of the tunnel," Jessica continued softly, staring fixedly at Mr. Fowler.

"A light," Mr. Fowler repeated. "Which end of the tunnel?"

"Which end?" Jessica frowned. "Um, the left end," she said, wondering if it made a difference.

"The left end." Mr. Fowler yawned. "Always good to be sure."

Lila snickered.

Jessica sighed. "Concentrate on the light," she instructed Mr. Fowler. "See it get bigger and brighter until it fills the tunnel with a warm glow."

"A warm glow," Mr. Fowler said. His voice sounded far away.

Jessica took a deep breath. "If you can hear me, bark like a dog," she ordered.

Mr. Fowler lifted up his head. "Arf, arf!" he barked, and then he smiled proudly. "Like that?" he asked.

Jessica made a face. Maybe he wasn't really under after all. "When I say the word *now,* you will discover that everything tastes sweet," she said softly. "Now."

Mr. Folder licked a finger. "Tastes just like sugar," he remarked. "Mmm, mmm, good!"

Oh, forget it, Jessica thought. There were two possibilities: Either Mr. Fowler was just humoring her, or else he was too anxious to please.

Or maybe there was a third possibility: that she needed work on putting people under. Much as she hated to admit it, she suspected that this explanation might be true. She folded her arms and considered. *Tapping Your Inner Powers* wasn't any help.

But Dr. Q might be.

She grinned to herself. And what better way to get in touch with Dr. Q than through her sister, the skeptic?

"Are there any more commands?" Mr. Fowler asked hopefully. "Hypnosis makes me so tired I can hardly think straight." He yawned again.

Jessica sighed.

"No," she said aloud. "Wake up! We're done."

Just as I thought, she told herself as Mr. Fowler sat up and stretched. *He didn't even wait for me to snap my fingers!*

Six

◇

Elizabeth grinned. It was Friday after school, and she was going over her list of questions to ask Dr. Q during the interview they'd scheduled for four-thirty that afternoon. Some of the questions were real killers, she thought.

"'Question number eight,'" she read aloud, although she was the only person in the *Sixers* office. "'If you're really psychic, why don't you buy the winning lottery ticket every week?'"

Elizabeth sat back, a smile of satisfaction on her face. If Dr. Q really could tell the future, she'd use that ability to make lots of money, wouldn't she? Of course she would. Jessica would, that was for sure. Elizabeth tapped her pencil against the desk. She wanted to see how Dr. Q would wriggle her way out of that one. Or out of the other incisive questions on her list.

The door opened. Startled, Elizabeth looked up from her list to see Bruce walk in, swaggering as usual. "Are you ever in luck," he proclaimed, crossing the room and clapping his hand familiarly on her shoulder.

Ugh. Elizabeth squirmed out from under his hand. "What do you want, Bruce?" she asked. "I'm kind of busy just now, and—"

"I, the great Bruce, am here to save the day!" Bruce announced. He struck a pose that Elizabeth thought was probably supposed to be triumphant and macho, but to her eyes it only looked silly. "You—yes, *you*—are coming with me to a totally awesome movie Saturday night."

Elizabeth sighed. She could think of nothing she would like less than attending a movie with Bruce. *He's probably just trying to outmacho Todd*, she told herself. "What movie, Bruce?" she asked, although she thought she could probably guess.

Bruce's eyes lit up. "The latest movie starring the greatest actor in the history of the universe—Arnold Weissenhammer!"

Elizabeth shuddered. "No, thanks, Bruce," she said. The idea of Arnold Weissenhammer being the greatest actor in the history of the universe! She rolled her eyes. *Well, maybe if the only people in the universe were Arnold Weissenhammer and Bruce Patman!*

"No?" Bruce stared at her in astonishment. "The kid says no to Arnold Weissenhammer?"

"No, thanks," Elizabeth repeated, more firmly

this time. Actually, she was saying no to Bruce Patman, but she decided not to tell him that. "Bruce, if you'll excuse me—"

"Aw, c'mon!" Bruce put his hands on his hips. "Don't tell me you've got a date already!"

"As a matter of fact, yes," Elizabeth said testily. "And we're not going to see any shoot-'em-up movie. We're going to see—"

"Who's the lucky guy?" Bruce demanded. "Wilkins, I bet. Todd Wilkins, right? That wimp?"

Wimp? "Get out of the office," Elizabeth ordered. She stood up and pointed, just in case Bruce was too stupid to find the door. What right did Bruce have to call Todd a wimp anyway? "Out, now!"

"OK, OK!" Bruce protested. "You're sure about this, huh? Give me a call if you change your mind, all right?"

Elizabeth gave Bruce a shove. "To tell you the truth, Bruce," she said, propelling him quickly out the door, "I wouldn't go out with you if you were the last guy on earth!"

Bruce smirked. "Your loss!" he said grandly.

With a deep sigh, Elizabeth returned to her list of questions for Dr. Q. She had a new one. "Question number nine," she muttered to herself, writing furiously. "If you're really psychic, how come you didn't hypnotize Bruce out of being the total jerk that he is?"

It would be a public service, she thought. If Dr. Q could really hypnotize people, she had no business letting Bruce run loose the way he was. If Dr. Q could do what she said she could do, she had a responsibility to make Bruce a nice person for a change. To make him a human being. Even if that meant making him do something out of character—

Wait a minute.

Elizabeth sat very still. On the stage the day before, Dr. Q had told Bruce to think about doing something out of character.

And asking Elizabeth Wakefield out was *totally* out of character for Bruce.

Which meant—

"Coincidence," Elizabeth muttered to herself, picking up her pencil again.

Wasn't it?

"Elizabeth! Wait up!"

Elizabeth had just left the school building to start the short walk to Dr. Q's office. She swung around to see Amy running up to her.

"Hi!" Elizabeth called out. "What's up?"

"Oh, nothing," Amy panted, running to Elizabeth's side. "Where are you going?"

"To see the not-so-mysterious Dr. Q," Elizabeth said with a smile. "I have an interview scheduled with her today. It ought to be interesting."

"Oh, yeah?" Amy's eyes opened very wide as she fell into step with Elizabeth.

"What are you doing still hanging around school?" Elizabeth wanted to know. Amy usually headed straight home on Friday afternoons—or else she and Elizabeth and their friend Maria Slater all went to Casey's ice cream parlor together.

Amy turned slightly pink. "Oh, um, nothing. You know." She kicked a pebble. "Just, um, hanging out." Her voice sounded unusually bright.

"Well, I hope you have fun," Elizabeth said. She couldn't wait to see the expression on Dr. Q's face when she sprang question number four on her: "If you're really psychic, tell me what my sister's favorite color is!" She turned left at the intersection. "See you later!"

Amy followed. "Um—Elizabeth?"

Elizabeth raised an eyebrow. "I thought you were hanging out," she said.

"Oh." Amy looked embarrassed. "Well—I'm, um, done hanging out, I guess. I'm, you know, going home."

"Home?" Elizabeth looked at Amy in surprise. "But you live that way, don't you?" She pointed to the right.

Amy took a deep breath. "I thought I'd go the long way today," she explained. "Because it's such a nice day out."

"It is?" Elizabeth looked up at the cloudy sky.

"Well, in fact," Amy said quickly, "I don't really have anything else to do this afternoon, and if you're going to interview Dr. Q, maybe I could, like, come too? I wouldn't bother you or anything," she added as Elizabeth opened her mouth to speak. "I'd just, you know, help you take notes and stuff."

Elizabeth nodded. "Sure, Amy. I'd love to have you."

"Oh, thanks!" Amy said, brightening up instantly. She skipped along beside Elizabeth, a grin on her face. "This is going to be so cool!" she crowed. "Imagine, us talking to a big-time hypnotist! I can't wait!"

Elizabeth grinned. It was a good idea to have Amy along, she decided. Amy was so enthusiastic, even if she thought hypnosis actually existed, and she really could help with the interview.

"I'm so glad I ran into you!" Amy was saying.

Hmmm. Frowning, Elizabeth took a close look at her friend. *I wonder if she really was "just hanging out" after school,* she thought. *Or if she was hoping to run into somebody who just happened to be on her way to Dr. Q's office.*

Like me!

"It looks ordinary enough," Amy said.

Elizabeth nodded. They stood outside a three-story office building. "Six Fountain Plaza," she read, squinting at the sign. "Offices of . . . let's see . . . a couple of dentists, an insurance agency—"

"And Dr. Q," Amy said, stabbing her finger at the last listing on the sign. "But I don't understand. Where are the six fountains?"

"The six fountains?" Elizabeth frowned. "What six fountains?"

"You know," Amy said, pushing a lock of hair behind her ear. "Six Fountain Plaza? So where are the six fountains?"

"Oh!" Elizabeth smiled. "That's the address. The street's called Fountain Plaza, and this is number six, that's all."

"Oops." Amy's cheeks turned red. "I'm so embarrassed!"

"Don't worry about it," Elizabeth said, waving her hand in the air. She was a little surprised that Dr. Q's address would be Fountain Plaza, though. She had expected something more mysterious. More showy. Like Black Cat Lane. Or Inner Powers Drive.

Or at least, she thought, *she ought to work in some old, creepy mansion somewhere.*

Elizabeth tucked her notebook under her arm, pushed the outer door open—and stared in astonishment.

"Hi, Lizzie!" Jessica said from inside the lobby. She yawned and looked lazily at her watch. "Thought you'd never get here," she said with a grin.

"What are *you* doing here?" Elizabeth demanded. She leaned against the heavy inner door that led to the offices. Somehow she thought she knew.

"I'm coming with you to the interview," Jessica announced proudly. "Don't bother to push open that door, by the way—it's locked. I'm going to learn all of Dr. Q's secrets."

Elizabeth sighed. *Just what I need—my sister along on this interview.* "What makes you think she'll tell you?" she asked, checking the inner door to make sure it was locked. But Jessica had been right. "And if you were really psychic, you wouldn't have to ask for her secrets. You'd simply read her mind."

"You have no idea how it works," Jessica said. "I just need practice, is all. The talent's there. All I have to do is learn some exercises to develop my ability." She stared hard at Elizabeth. "It's like playing tennis or something. You wouldn't expect somebody to become great without a coach."

"That makes sense," Amy agreed.

Elizabeth sighed again. "And if Dr. Q is really psychic, how come she hasn't let you in yet?" she asked. She gestured toward the doorbell marked simply *Q*. "I mean, why does she even have a doorbell? She should just *know* when someone comes to the door."

Jessica shrugged. "That's easy. Because she knew I was waiting for you. And now that we're all here—"

A metallic voice came through the intercom.

"Are you all ready?" Dr. Q asked. "Enter, please."

The inner door buzzed.

Elizabeth stood still, wondering how Dr. Q had known. But Jessica had already seized the handle and yanked the door open. "Coming?" she asked as Amy darted forward.

Elizabeth bit her lip. It was *her* interview. And she would have preferred it if Jessica had never shown up. But there was no use arguing with her sister once she had her mind set on something.

Might as well try to empty a lake with an eyedropper! she thought grimly as she followed Amy and Jessica through the door.

Seven

There's no mystery about how she knew we were there, Elizabeth told herself, sitting down on a soft couch in Dr. Q's office a few minutes later. There was a window that sort of faced the front entrance. *She was just watching out the window for us.* Although the window didn't have a really good view of the sidewalk, she had to admit.

Or maybe she heard us talking in the foyer. Yeah, that's probably it.

"This is so cool!" Jessica said. She whipped out a notebook of her own. "So how do you do it, huh?"

"And, um, maybe you could give us another demonstration," Amy said nervously in the background. "Like, getting rid of people's fears. I could volunteer."

Elizabeth sighed. "Um, Amy, if you don't

mind—I'm doing this interview, OK?"

Dr. Q was minus the turban, but her eyes were as sharp as ever. "Can I get you something to drink? Some fruit juice, perhaps? It helps cleanse the thoughts, you know."

"No, thanks," Jessica said importantly. "Now, about the watch that you used to hypnotize us yesterday—"

"Does fruit juice help get rid of people's fears?" Amy asked doubtfully.

"A glass of fruit juice would be just fine," Elizabeth said, wishing that Jessica and Amy hadn't come along. Then, remembering her manners, she added: "Please." *It'll give me a moment to think, at least,* she told herself as Dr. Q opened a small refrigerator in the corner of the office. "Cut it out," Elizabeth hissed to Jessica.

"Who, me?" Jessica put her hand to her chest and did her best to look innocent.

"If she could just give us a demonstration . . ." Amy's voice trailed off.

Elizabeth sighed. Yes, letting Amy and Jessica come along was starting to look like a bad idea. A really, really bad idea. Especially because Dr. Q could see that Jessica was wearing purple from head to toe. Well, to ankle anyway. Her shoes were black. Obviously Jessica's favorite color was purple. Dr. Q didn't have to be psychic at all to figure *that* out. "So much for question number four," she muttered, crossing out "What's my sister's favorite color?" with a vicious line.

Taking a deep breath, she glanced around the room. The office was full of candles—big candles and small candles, twisted candles and straight candles, pink candles and yellow candles. Some had gobs of wax clinging to their sides, while others looked as though they had never been burned.

Elizabeth's gaze swept on. Three robes hung on hooks near the door. One was purple, one red, and the third a shimmering bluish green. The far wall was decorated with five framed pencil drawings— a circle, a square, a star, some wavy lines, and a cross. The wallpaper had a strange design that Elizabeth finally decided was the letter *Q* repeated in several different sizes and styles. *Her monogram, probably,* she thought. On a nearby shelf Elizabeth could see a pile of beads, and there was a basket of fluorescent rocks at her feet.

No doubt about it—it was a little spooky. Spookier than the auditorium stage anyway. Elizabeth half wished she'd arranged to interview Dr. Q in the *Sixers* office instead.

"Here you are," Dr. Q said, handing Amy and Elizabeth glasses full of a liquid that reminded Elizabeth of blood. It was that color anyway. Carefully she sniffed it. It smelled all right, so she tasted it. *Hmmm. Not bad.*

"I don't poison the juice," Dr. Q said with a smile. "It's a mixture of several exotic fruits— guava, passion fruit, things like that."

Elizabeth nodded. It was certainly richer than

your everyday apple or orange juice. "Thanks for agreeing to this interview, Dr. Q," she began, but her voice was squeakier than she'd intended. She cleared her throat. She wasn't nervous or anything, she was sure. "I mean—"

"My pleasure," Dr. Q said with a smile, settling into an easy chair. She was wearing a long flowing skirt with a peasant-type blouse, and her long hair was done up in a bun at the back of her head.

"Um—" Elizabeth said with a laugh, consulting her notebook. *The first question,* she thought, licking her lips. *The one that Mr. Bowman says can make or break an interview.* "Um, Dr. Q, let's be completely honest with each other. We both know there's no such thing as hypnosis, don't we?"

"I beg your pardon?" Dr. Q leaned forward, her eyes twinkling.

Elizabeth gulped. The question had sounded a lot more important and, well, *penetrating* when Dr. Q wasn't actually there to answer it. And when her voice was firmer and more in control. "There's no such thing as hypnosis," Elizabeth repeated weakly, wishing she'd started with a different question. "Right?"

"Of *course* there's such a thing as hypnosis," Jessica interrupted. "Dr. Q hypnotized us only yesterday. I remember every single second of it. Are you a total idiot or something?"

"I think hypnosis works," Amy chimed in. "At least where people's fears are concerned. Right, Dr. Q?"

"Will you two please shut up?" Elizabeth

snapped. Her stomach was churning. "Dr. Q, tell me the truth, please. Is there such a thing as hypnosis?"

It seemed like a different question from what she'd planned, somehow, and Elizabeth wished she'd asked it more confidently. The way Amy's mother would have. But it was too late now. She sat up straight and poised her pencil over the paper.

Dr. Q smiled. "Hypnosis exists," she said. "I can't say that we understand the process very well, but of course it's real."

"But—" Elizabeth bit her lip. "Isn't it just a trick?"

"Of course not," Jessica interrupted with a loud sigh. "We've been through this a million times, Lizzie. It's real, like it said in the book. You just have to know what you're doing."

"For fears it's real," Amy said timidly.

"A trick?" Dr. Q frowned at Elizabeth. "What sort of a trick are you talking about?"

"Well—you know." Elizabeth couldn't quite meet Dr. Q's eyes. "Like telling somebody that they'll taste something sweet, and then putting sugar all over something that they touch. Things like that."

"Ah." The smile returned to Dr. Q's face. "There may indeed be tricksters who treat hypnosis as a joke. But that does not mean hypnosis is not real. I, for one, would never play a trick like that."

"See?" Jessica crowed. "What did I tell you?"

Elizabeth glared at Jessica, then turned back to Dr. Q. "Says hypn. is real," she scrawled in her notebook, which was balanced precariously on her knee. She hoped she could read her writing later on. "Oh," she said helplessly. Dr. Q had sounded quite positive. "Are you, um, sure?"

Dr. Q only nodded.

"This is silly," Jessica complained. "I want to learn how to do hypnosis. Do you *have* to use candles, Dr. Q?"

"Maybe you could do a demonstration," Amy suggested again. "Like, on me. You could get rid of my fears. If I had any."

"Dr. Q," Elizabeth said, scanning the list of questions to find a good one, "if you really are psychic, why don't you make a lot of money on the lottery, or the horse races, or the stock market, or something like that?" She took a deep breath. *There. That question sounded pretty good anyway.*

Dr. Q nodded again. "It's a fair question," she said softly. With a start, Elizabeth realized the doctor was looking right into her eyes. "Let me answer you with a question. Do you have an adviser to your school newspaper?"

"Yes," Elizabeth said slowly. "Mr. Bowman. But what does he have to do with—"

"It's so *obvious*," Jessica said, rolling her eyes.

Dr. Q held up her hand. She had unusually long fingers, Elizabeth noticed. "Your Mr. Bowman has some experience with the news, I take it?"

If you were really psychic, you'd know that, Elizabeth thought, but she decided not to say it. "Yeah," she admitted. "I mean, he worked for a newspaper for a year or two, I think. And he writes articles for a weekly paper."

Dr. Q stared fixedly at Elizabeth's face. "Most journalists are not rich, but some are. Mr. Bowman could be a well-known, well-off reporter if he chose. So why doesn't he pursue journalism?"

"Because—um, because—" Pulling away from Dr. Q's gaze (it wasn't easy), Elizabeth looked to Amy for help. "Because—"

"Because he doesn't want to?" Amy guessed. "Because he'd rather teach kids to be journalists?"

"Precisely," Dr. Q said. "He has the talent, but he prefers to use it for other ends. I do the same." She spread her arms out wide. "I am careful about how I use my powers, my dear. I do not use them to enrich myself; instead, I educate others less gifted than I about the wonders—and dangers—of the psychic world."

"Like I said, Lizzie," Jessica said with a long sigh.

Elizabeth took a deep breath. "Um—OK," she said softly, writing down what Dr. Q had said.

It made sense in a weird kind of a way.

But she couldn't help feeling that there was something wrong with Dr. Q's argument.

Jessica sighed impatiently, looked pointedly at the clock (monogrammed with a Q) on the wall in front of her, and folded her arms in front of her chest. This interview was going nowhere fast.

"But what about making Bruce Patman less of a

jerk?" Elizabeth said, staring down at the notebook in her lap. "Don't you have to, like, make him a nice guy?"

"I beg your pardon?" Dr. Q looked confused.

Jessica examined her fingernails. Elizabeth was sounding more and more incoherent, and anyway, Dr. Q's answers were right on the mark. Plus hypnosis existed and that was a fact, so why would anyone care what Elizabeth wrote? Jessica's own questions were more important, that was for sure.

"What I mean is," Elizabeth began desperately, "you told Bruce Patman to, you know, imagine himself doing something that would be out of character for him, and, um—" She frowned. "That is—well— he's so arrogant and stuff, and why didn't you just tell him to cut out being arrogant for the rest of his life? I mean, if he was really hypnotized."

Jessica couldn't stand it any longer. "If I could ask a question—" she began loudly.

"Jessica!" Elizabeth bit her lip and glared at her sister.

"The important thing is that I learn how to do this stuff," Jessica shot back. "*That's* what's important, not your silly newspaper." She felt a tiny pang of guilt. She knew how seriously her sister took her journalism career.

But if I'm ever going to develop my psychic powers, now's the time, Jessica told herself firmly, overriding that guilty feeling. "So how about it, Dr. Q? Some tips, please." With a flourish she opened her notebook to a blank page and held her pencil expectantly over the paper.

Dr. Q smiled, but her eyes pierced Jessica's own. "Elizabeth, the answer to your question is that hypnosis cannot make the world a perfect place," she said softly. "Your friend Bruce may be, as you put it, a jerk, but hypnosis will not stop that." Dr. Q shrugged, her hair shimmering over her peasant blouse. "If he wished to change, then perhaps I could help him."

"But if somebody wanted to overcome their fears," Amy went on hurriedly, "you could do something?"

Dr. Q nodded. "Yes. If they truly wanted to overcome those fears."

Bo-ring. "As I was saying," Jessica interrupted loudly, "the subject here isn't fears and it isn't Bruce Patman. It's hypnosis. So what's the secret, Dr. Q, huh?" She knew she was being just a little rude, but she didn't care. If she could only learn to hypnotize people, maybe she'd even hypnotize Elizabeth into asking better questions on interviews such as this.

"But—" Elizabeth raised her hand.

Then again, maybe not. "Please, Dr. Q?" Jessica begged, flashing the doctor her best smile.

A star pendant around Dr. Q's neck sparkled in the light. She sighed deeply. "Very well," she agreed. "To be a hypnotist, one must first be in tune with one's own innermost thoughts and feelings."

"Check," Jessica said, busily writing it down. *That's easy. I'm the most in-tune person I know!*

"Second," Dr. Q went on, holding up a long finger, "the hypnotist must achieve a state of absolute calm."

"Absolute calm," Jessica wrote. She suspected she might have misspelled *absolute,* but she didn't care. *That'll be easy too,* she told herself happily. *I'm always calm.* She looked up. "But *how* do you—"

"Hypnosis is an art," Dr. Q went on, rearranging the folds of her skirt. "I can give you some suggestions about developing your skills, but there is one thing you must remember."

"Which is?" Jessica said, wondering when they would get to the good stuff.

"Just this." Dr. Q leaned forward and fixed Jessica with her hardest stare yet. "Hypnosis is not a toy, never a toy. It is a tool, and a powerful but dangerous one." She folded her hands neatly in her lap. "Do not play with it. Do you understand?"

"Sure, sure," Jessica grunted, not bothering to write it down. She waved her hand in the air dismissively. "Now, about this elevator business—"

"She said *some people* fake it," Elizabeth argued. The twins were on their way home from Dr. Q's office, with Amy trailing dejectedly a few feet behind them.

"She said she *didn't* fake it," Jessica shot back. "So that means—"

"She just said she never pulled the sugar trick," Elizabeth pointed out. "There are all kinds of other tricks she could have pulled, and you know it."

"Not Dr. Q," Jessica responded stubbornly. "She didn't say a *word* about faking when she was telling me how to hypnotize people. Not one single solitary *word*."

Amy sighed. It sounded to her as if both Elizabeth and Jessica had gotten what they'd wanted out of seeing Dr. Q. Elizabeth was still convinced that hypnosis didn't exist, and Jessica was still positive that it did.

And as for herself—well, she'd blown it. Her one chance. She'd casually brought up the idea of doing a demonstration a couple of times, but Jessica or Elizabeth had always gotten in there first and moved the conversation away from demonstrations.

And from fears.

Amy sighed again. Her stomach hurt at the very thought of the helicopter ride. *Just over a week away.* She felt her throat tighten. *I won't be able to go anyway,* she thought grimly, *because I won't be able to eat and I won't be able to breathe, and they'll put me in the hospital. And I'll never get to be on TV.*

"You were not faking yesterday," Jessica said.

"I was so!" Elizabeth's eyes blazed. "And so were you, I bet. I just bet!"

"No possible way," Jessica said with dignity. "And you were really hypnotized. I could practically—"

"I was *totally* faking," Elizabeth interrupted. Her cheeks were turning slightly pink. "It was pathetic, what that woman was trying to put over on us."

Jessica's eyes flashed. "I'm telling you, 'that woman' had powers," she said darkly.

"So prove it," Elizabeth challenged.

Jessica frowned. "Huh?"

Elizabeth glared at her twin. "Hypnotize me," she dared Jessica. "Hypnotize *Amy*. Hypnotize *Bruce*. Hypnotize everybody! Bet you can't."

"What are you talking about?" Jessica snorted.

"Let's see you hypnotize us," Elizabeth repeated. "At our house tomorrow. You invite some friends, and I'll invite some friends, and you hypnotize us all. *If* you can."

Amy drew in her breath. *Yes!* she thought. She focused on sending thought waves to Jessica. She wasn't sure Jessica could pull it off, but it was worth a try. *Do it—do it—do it—*

"You're serious?" Jessica's eyebrows shot up.

"You bet!" Elizabeth snapped.

Jessica grinned. "Then we've got a deal!" she said, extending her hand for Elizabeth to shake.

"Wakefield house, Elizabeth speaking."

Todd's mouth felt suddenly dry. He'd carefully written down exactly what he was going to say, but now that Elizabeth was actually on the phone, he didn't seem to be able to say it. "Um," he said into the receiver, stalling for time, "is Elizabeth there, please?"

The girl on the line giggled. "This *is* Elizabeth."

"Oh, right." Todd could have smacked himself

on the head. *Duh! She even said so, you loser!* "Um, this is Todd. Wilkins."

"Oh!" There was a sudden silence. Todd gripped the receiver tightly, afraid for an instant that she would hang up. "Hi, Todd!" Elizabeth said after a moment.

She sounds enthusiastic anyway. Todd's eyes flicked down to the next line of his prepared script. "Um—I was just calling to remind you about our date tomorrow. In case you'd forgotten," he said. He licked his lips. Maybe he shouldn't have sounded so tentative. Confident and strong, that was the ticket. Like Patman. "I mean—"

"Of course I haven't forgotten," Elizabeth assured him. "Thanks for calling. I really, really appreciate it."

"Really?" Todd cleared his throat. That hadn't sounded very confident. "I mean, great. Well, see you tomorrow." He started to hang up.

"Todd—wait!"

Startled, Todd nearly dropped the phone. "What is it?" he asked nervously.

"My sister's having a hypnosis party, if you can believe it," Elizabeth said with a little laugh. "At two o'clock tomorrow. Why don't you come if you can?"

"A hypnosis party?" Todd repeated, not sure if he'd heard correctly.

"That's right," Elizabeth said. "She thinks she can hypnotize people, ha ha. How'd you like to be a guinea pig?"

Todd thought quickly. Actually, it didn't sound like a bad idea at all. There would probably be lots of other people, so he could hide if he got too nervous around Elizabeth, and hanging out with Elizabeth in the afternoon would be good practice for their date later that night, and—

And his heart was still beating awfully fast. So a little hypnosis might help him be a little less nervous.

"Sure," he agreed. And then, hoping he wasn't coming on too strong, he added casually: "I mean, I'll try to make it."

"Great!" Elizabeth exclaimed. *She sounds excited*, Todd thought. *Maybe she really does like me.* "Oh, and if you want to, why don't you bring a friend?" she added.

"A friend?" Todd asked stupidly. A picture of Bruce popped into his mind. Bruce, who'd scoffed at the idea that a guy might actually like a girl. Bruce, who'd practically dared him to ask Elizabeth on a date.

It would be a great opportunity to show Bruce just how tight he and Elizabeth really were, he decided.

Eight

◇

"I can't believe I'm missing the big game for *this*," Bruce complained. "I mean, the only reason I'm here at all is because Wilkins called me up and told me all about how you were doing this séance thing and we'd get to watch you fall flat on your face—"

"Oh, I did not either," Todd protested, turning faintly pink.

"It's not a *séance*," Jessica interrupted frostily, fixing Bruce with a look. Then she glared at Todd too, for good measure. "It's a hypnosis demonstration, and you know it." She adjusted the gigantic purple towel she was using for a robe. "If you would all please take your seats," she said in what she hoped was a mysterious voice. She stared at Amy, trying to match Dr. Q's penetrating glare. "We need to get started."

"Hey, Jessica!" Janet Howell called from across the room. "I've got an extra ticket to the circus next Saturday. Want to go?"

Jessica forgot her mystic pose and frowned. "The *circus?*"

Janet made an impatient noise deep in her throat. "Not elephants and seals and clowns. Not *that* kind of circus, duh." Her eyes sparkled. "These are, like, gymnasts. Hot guys soaring through the air and pumping rings and stuff like that?"

Jessica nodded, thrilled to be asked. "Sure, Janet!"

"Hey, Bruce!" Lila said brightly. "I'm taking bets. How long before Jessica messes up?"

"Two minutes," Bruce said. "The Angels-Twins game is on *national TV*. And it started *half an hour* ago."

"Two minutes?" Lila repeated. "I was going to guess five, but maybe I'll say three."

Jessica choked back a reply. *My so-called best friend—ha!* She stared intently at Lila, sending her a telepathic message to shut up.

"She tried to hypnotize me, you know," Lila said brightly. "Of course it didn't work. I'm much more psychic than she is."

"If the Angels lose today—" Bruce began.

Jessica seized her spiral pendant and rapped angrily on the table with it. "Please take your seats," she commanded.

This time it worked. The kids sat. Even Lila flounced into her seat, having shut up at last. *Good.* Jessica hoped it was the ESP message that had done it. Maybe it proved she really was psychic.

She took a deep breath and watched the flickering candles on the table in front of her. There were eight of them, just as Dr. Q had prescribed. Unless she had really said eighteen. Jessica had to admit that her notes weren't absolutely clear on the subject. Next to the candles was a box of fluorescent stones, just like Dr. Q's. Well, maybe not *just* like Dr. Q's. In fact, they were a bunch of pebbles sprayed with luminous paint.

She dimmed the lights and began swinging her spiral pendant back and forth. "Watch the rhythm of my hand," she intoned. "Relax and watch. Relax and watch. . . ."

Bruce yawned. Amy was staring fixedly in front of her.

Jessica felt her heart beginning to race. "You are getting sleepy," she chanted, swinging the charm faster through the air. "You are getting sleepy. . . ."

She hoped that the glassy-eyed stares she was seeing on the faces of the other kids were the beginnings of hypnotic trances and not just expressions of boredom.

Todd felt his eyelids beginning to shut. *Good*, he thought. He hadn't expected that Jessica would have this kind of talent, but it was a nice surprise. He stole a quick glance at Elizabeth. As always, his heart leaped. He just wished he could find the words to tell her so.

Actually, Todd realized, it wasn't so much the

words that were the problem. It was more that he needed the courage. . . .

He yawned widely. To tell the truth, he thought fuzzily, he was kind of looking forward to . . . being . . . hypnotized. . . .

Being—

Hypnotized—

"You are very sleepy," Jessica chanted.

Amy concentrated on relaxing. She wiggled her toes, but they felt heavy, almost leaden. Her eyes had shut. She could almost feel herself floating off the chair.

"You are *very* sleepy," Jessica continued.

Amy yawned, but air didn't seem to fill her lungs. She felt strangely tired, and yet peaceful. She forced herself to think about helicopters. For half a second the thought didn't terrify her.

So this is what it's like, she thought happily. *And the next time I open my eyes, I'll never be scared again!*

Strange, Elizabeth thought with a yawn. She just couldn't seem to keep her eyes open. The sound of her sister's voice was persistent—something about elevators. Or maybe escalators.

She yawned again and tried to push her eyelids open.

Of course, she was just tired. She'd been up late the night before. That was all . . . wasn't it?

Jessica scanned the row of glassy stares in front of

her. *This is it*, she thought nervously. The candles flickered, casting eerie shadows on the walls. *It's do or die.*

Her fingers fumbled for the slips of paper she'd passed around earlier in the afternoon. She'd asked the kids to list their greatest fear. A few of them were obviously jokes. *Aaron isn't really afraid of getting squashed inside a humongous loaf of bread*, she thought irritably.

But a few sounded right. Janet had written "Mice and spiders, yuck!" And silly old Amy had written "flying" in very small letters.

The only sound was the noise of a bunch of kids breathing slowly, regularly, and evenly.

"Amy, listen to me," Jessica said, chanting in a calming, singsongy voice. "You will never again fear flying." She turned to Janet. "And Janet, you will never again fear mice. Or spiders."

Silence.

Jessica adjusted her robe. She hoped they'd heard. "If you understand, raise your right hand," she ordered.

No one moved a muscle.

Oops. Jessica ran her tongue along her upper lip. "Um—when you wake up, you will remember what has been said," she commanded. "You will remember—"

"Oh, no!" Bruce piped up from the audience. "Two-run homer for the Twins!"

He's listening to the ball game! Jessica thought angrily. And now that she looked closely, she could see a tiny earphone wedged into Bruce's right ear. "Shhh!" she ordered.

Startled, Bruce pulled the earphone out. The radio announcer's voice blared across the room. "The Twins now lead by a score of two to one—the identical score they won by yester—"

This was never going to work. "Shhh!" Jessica repeated in her fiercest voice, and Bruce snapped the radio off.

Jessica turned her attention back to Janet and Amy, hoping the interruption wouldn't be a problem. "If you have heard, raise your right hand," she said again. To her surprise, both girls raised their hands straight up in the air.

Well, what do you know? Jessica's eyes lit up. *I guess I must be doing something right after all!*

She only hoped her next victim wouldn't be as difficult.

Jessica stood up and examined her hypnotized sister. She *looked* hypnotized, at least—she was completely glassy-eyed. Jessica's lips curved into a smile. *It's payback time.* She was going to program Elizabeth to think that Jessica Wakefield was the greatest person the world had ever known.

"You are truly sleepy," she chanted. "When you wake up, you will love and admire the greatest person on earth—" She paused for effect, enjoying the moment. "The one and only—"

"Bruce Patman!" Ellen Riteman's angry voice came out of the darkness just as Jessica said, "Jessica Wakefield!"

"Sorry," Bruce grumbled. "How was I supposed to know that was your foot?"

Jessica glared in Bruce's direction. Twice now Bruce had disrupted the whole thing! She wished that Todd hadn't invited him. "Shhh!" she hissed.

"Well, you should have looked!" Ellen complained.

"What's it doing under my chair, huh?" Bruce argued.

"Shhh!" Things were going downhill fast. *At least Elizabeth's still out,* Jessica reassured herself. She leaned closer to her dazed sister. "If you have heard me, raise your right hand," she commanded.

Elizabeth's hand shot up. Way up.

And it doesn't even look faked, Jessica told herself, wondering if maybe she was really on to something. Her eyes gleamed. "Put your hand down," she told her twin.

Elizabeth's hand sank slowly. Jessica turned to Lila. *We'll see who's psychic and who isn't,* she thought. *And I'll teach you to place bets on how soon the Incredible Madame Jessica will mess up.* She was going to enjoy this one especially.

"In a past life," Jessica said in her most soothing voice, "you were a duck."

No one spoke.

"A duck," Jessica repeated. "Let me hear you quack, Lila."

Lila lifted her head. "Quack!" she repeated dutifully.

Jessica could hardly believe her good luck. That

is, her amazing talent. She studied Lila carefully. Yup, Lila definitely looked different than she had the night she'd been pretending to be hypnotized. "Every time you see the principal of our school, Mr. Clark," Jessica went on, "you will remember your inner duckness, and you will only quack." *Detention city, here we come!*

Lila mumbled something under her breath. It sounded vaguely like "Yes, master."

Jessica felt a surge of power. Somehow Lila's words didn't sound fake this time. "Who is the principal?"

"Mr. Quack," Lila replied.

Jessica smiled. "Very good! Very, very good. Now, everybody, wake up!" She snapped her fingers.

Slowly eyes opened all over the room. Kids yawned and stretched, while Jessica watched with sweaty palms, waiting to see what would happen.

"Well, that obviously didn't work," Lila said. "I feel just fine. Anybody who said more than three minutes—"

Just wait, Lila, Jessica thought, wondering if she should ask her friend to name the principal. *No— better to hold off till Monday.* "How do you feel about flying, Amy?" she asked.

"Flying?" Amy made a face. "No, thanks! But Janet will hold my hand if I go up in a plane, right?"

"Janet?" Jessica blinked. *Since when are Janet and Amy friends?*

"I've got a better idea," Janet said, coming over

to pat Amy's shoulder. "If worse comes to worst, I'll just go up in your place."

"Hey, yeah!" Amy brightened. "They'd never be able to tell the difference, would they?"

"They wouldn't?" Confused, Jessica glanced from Janet to Amy and back. "But you two don't look anything alike."

"Of course we do," Amy said, slipping her arm through Janet's. "After all, we're identical twins. Aren't we, sister dear?"

"We sure are," Janet agreed, ruffling Amy's hair affectionately.

Uh-oh. Jessica pursed her lips. "But you guys aren't twins," she said slowly. "You aren't even re-lated." She gave a nervous laugh. "This is a joke, right?"

"Certainly not," Janet sniffed.

Amy's lip curled. "No possible way," she agreed. "We're identical twins, down to the toe-nails." The two girls laughed.

Jessica felt a dull ache in the pit of her stomach. Janet and Amy wouldn't joke like that, would they? And they certainly wouldn't joke together. They didn't even particularly like each other. Had she done this somehow? She licked her lips, trying to think.

"Why don't you turn on the game again, Bruce?" Aaron asked.

The game. Jessica swallowed hard. She cast her mind back to when she'd put Amy and Janet under. What had she said? *When you wake up, you will remember this.* That was it. And then—

She frowned. And then Bruce had yelled something about somebody hitting a home run in the game. Someone for the—

Uh-oh. The Twins. And then—Jessica took a deep breath—*the announcer used the word* identical. *Something about "the identical score."*

Which was what Amy and Janet had heard. So they thought they were identical twins. The reality hit Jessica like a ton of bricks.

"I'm *so* glad I have an identical twin," Amy told Janet.

"Me too," Janet said dreamily. "I don't know *what* I'd do without one."

Jessica sighed. *Well, it's not the end of the world,* she reminded herself. In fact, it was kind of neat to have so much power.

"See, it's just like I said," Bruce remarked near Jessica's elbow. "Totally dorky. Hypnosis, yeah, right. Some great demonstration, huh, Elizabeth?"

Jessica's pulse quickened. There was something weird about the way Bruce had said her sister's name. She turned to locate her twin.

"Whatever you say, Bruce," Elizabeth said, smiling up at Bruce. "You certainly have the most brilliant ideas!"

"Yeah, well," Bruce said importantly. He took a step toward Elizabeth and put his arm gently on her shoulder. "That's just the kind of guy I am."

"I know." Elizabeth's smile grew bigger. "I think

I've always kind of known that, Bruce."

Jessica blinked in astonishment. *She isn't pushing him away!* she thought. If anything, Elizabeth was leaning closer to Bruce, burrowing into his arm. "Elizabeth?" she croaked, swallowing hard. *My sister? With Bruce—ahem—Patman?*

"I'm sorry it didn't work, Jess," Elizabeth said, gazing dreamily at Bruce.

Jessica could feel her jaw dropping open. She stared in astonishment as her sister reached up to stroke Bruce's cheek. Again she thought back.

It must have been Ellen, she decided. *Bruce put his chair leg down on Ellen's foot, and she yelled his name just as I was telling Elizabeth to think I was the greatest person in the world!*

"Hey, um, Elizabeth?" Todd was suddenly at Elizabeth's side, looking uncomfortable. "What time should I, um, pick you up tonight?"

"Tonight?" A perplexed frown spread across Elizabeth's face. "Do you know what this is about?" she asked Bruce.

Bruce shook his head and pretended to yawn.

"Bruce and I are going to a really cool movie tonight," Elizabeth explained to Todd.

"The Arnold Weissenhammer flick," Bruce added casually.

"You're what?" The blood seemed to drain from Todd's face. "You're going to see Arnold Weissenhammer? With—him?"

"That's right," Elizabeth went on, smiling gently

at Todd. "But I'm sure we'll see you around."

"Elizabeth!" Todd protested, biting his lip.

Bruce stepped forward and pivoted so that his back was between Todd and Elizabeth. "Later, guy," he said dismissively.

For a second Todd stared over Bruce's shoulder, eyes pleading with Elizabeth. But when Elizabeth didn't respond, Todd clenched his fists and stomped up the steps, not even saying good-bye.

Jessica felt sorry for Todd as she watched him leave. But not much. *So things got turned around,* she thought. *So Janet and Amy didn't get over their fears, and Elizabeth thinks the wrong person is the greatest thing on earth.*

So what?

Jessica grinned. She'd proven to herself that she had the skills to do it. All she needed was practice—and a little more experience, so that minor things wouldn't go wrong the way they had that day.

Jessica the psychic. Jessica the hypnotist.

Her eyes glistened in the dim light of the room.

Today, Sweet Valley. Tomorrow, the world!

Nine

◇

"Well, buddy, you know how it is," Bruce said into the phone. He chuckled. "Just gotta snap my fingers, and the girls come running."

Todd had been home for about two hours, but he was still fuming. It was all he could do not to scream. He had thought of lots of really interesting things to call Bruce. *Toad*, *worm*, and *mushroom breath* were some of the nicer ones. But the word he kept coming back to was one he'd learned in English class. An old-fashioned word. The word *cad*.

He wasn't sure, but he thought a cad was someone who went around stealing other guys' girlfriends.

Like some jerk he could mention.

"Hey, are you still there?" Bruce demanded into the phone.

"I'm still here, Bruce," Todd snapped. Ever since

he'd gotten home from the Wakefields', he'd been wondering whom he should blame. Elizabeth had really been hypnotized, he reasoned, so it wasn't her fault. He'd finally decided that the best target was Bruce. So he'd called up Booger Brain to yell at him. "You know, I really wanted to go out with Elizabeth tonight!"

"Yeah?" Bruce didn't sound as though he cared. "That's life. You should have asked her."

"I *did* ask her," Todd said, struggling to keep himself under control. "And you just horned in, which you had no right to do, and—"

"Hey, calm down," Bruce interrupted with a laugh. "Yeah, I remember something like that. Some discussion on the basketball court. But as I remember, you weren't doing a thing about it. Not a single, solitary thing."

"I did so!" Todd was steaming. "I asked her! And she said yes. In the cafeteria! Remember? You knew it, Bruce!"

"Did I?" Bruce said carelessly. "Hey, that's the way the cookie crumbles, kiddo."

Todd could scarcely believe his ears. "But you said you couldn't even be bothered with girls!" he protested. "I was *there*. I *heard* you, Bruce!"

Bruce laughed again. "Well, I couldn't let you get ahead of me in the girl department. Anyway, that was then, this is now. And Elizabeth's pretty cool, know what I mean?"

Todd's eyes flashed. He *did* know exactly

what Bruce meant. That was the problem.

"I hope she turns into a pumpkin!" he shouted.

Elizabeth narrowed her eyes and stared at her reflection in her full-length mirror. Nice skirt. Check. Hair brushed. Check. Purse slung over her left shoulder. Check.

Or maybe it would look better over her right shoulder . . .

"E-liz-a-beth!" Her older brother, Steven, was shouting at her from downstairs.

Elizabeth sighed. Steven could be such a pain sometimes. "Come on up if you want to talk!" she called back down.

"Phone for you!" Steven yelled. "Some guy named Bruce. He wants to know when he should pick you up."

Bruce. Elizabeth smiled in anticipation of their date. It was funny how she couldn't recall liking him very much before that afternoon. She cast her mind back, wondering what had happened to make her fall for him in such a big way.

"Earth to Elizabeth!" Steven shouted.

"Tell him six-thirty, please," Elizabeth answered. She turned back to the mirror and adjusted her right sleeve. *Six-thirty. Less than an hour.*

Bruce was cute, all right. Still, she couldn't remember noticing his great personality. But he had to have one.

Otherwise she wouldn't be going out with him. Right?

*   *   *

Todd set his jaw and dialed. The last time he'd punched in this particular number, he'd been unbelievably nervous. This time he wasn't nervous so much as mad. He checked his watch. Six thirty-five.

"Hello?"

The voice sounded like the voice of his dreams, but it was just a shade off. "Jessica?" he asked, surprised at how strong his own voice sounded.

"Speaking," Jessica Wakefield answered.

Todd took a deep breath. "Listen, this is Todd. Um, Wilkins," he added in case Jessica didn't remember. "I, um, have to know something. Did your sister go out with you-know-who?" He didn't trust himself to say the name of the world's number-one sleazebag.

"Oh. Hi, Todd." Jessica didn't sound exactly thrilled. "They just left, as a matter of fact. Bruce rented a limo."

A limo. Great. Todd bit his lip, not wanting to think of his girlfriend in a limo with Mr. Slime. "Do you know where they were going?" He thought he remembered, but he needed to be sure.

Jessica laughed. "The Weissenhammer movie, duh. *Blood, Guts, and Glory*. It's playing over at the mall."

"And this is all because you hypnotized them?" Todd asked incredulously.

"You bet!" Jessica said proudly. "Elizabeth anyway. No autographs, please. See, it happened like this—"

"Never mind, Jessica." Todd didn't care how it had happened as long as it unhappened in a hurry. "OK. Listen," he ordered. "I'm coming over to your house, and I'm going to pick you up, only it'll be in my dad's car, not in a limo, and we're going to the Valley Mall to see *Blood, Guts, Glory, and Car Crashes*. Can you be ready in five minutes?"

It was surprising how easy it was to ask out a girl you didn't really like, Todd reflected as he waited for Jessica's answer. And how hard it was to ask out a girl you really *did* like.

When Jessica didn't reply, Todd repeated, "I said, can you be ready in five minutes?"

"You mean go on a date?" Jessica asked in astonishment. "With *you?*"

Todd ground his teeth. "No. Not a date. I just want to, you know, keep an eye on your sister and her, um, friend." *I won't say he's her boyfriend,* he told himself, feeling that dull ache again. *Never her boyfriend!* "And it's easier if there's somebody with me."

Not to mention that my dad is ready to drive me over to your house, and I don't want to tell my dad that Elizabeth finked out on me.

"And besides," Todd went on, "if you hypnotized them, I bet you'd like to watch what's going on between them yourself."

"Oh." Jessica apparently hadn't considered this before. She drew in her breath slowly. "Well, now that you mention it," she said, "I guess I'm not doing much of anything else tonight, and the

Weissenhammer movie sounds pretty good. . . ."

Just say yes, Todd thought, feeling ready to scream.

"I guess so," Jessica finished in a bored voice. "If it really isn't, you know, a date. If you don't tell anybody."

"Promise. See you in five." Todd was about to slam down the phone, but Jessica interrupted.

"Todd?" she asked plaintively. "Don't you think maybe you could rent a limo too?"

On the screen a snappy red sports car dived left, rolled over six times, and hit a cement mixer inches from a yawning cliff. Elizabeth gasped and shut her eyes, but Bruce, next to her, guffawed.

"Can't wait to see that one," he said happily. "Hey, pass the popcorn."

Elizabeth handed Bruce the tub of popcorn he'd bought for them to share. "You mean this isn't the movie yet?" she asked.

Bruce shot her a look of irritation. "No way. It's the promo for the next one. Weissenhammer's so awesome! He churns out a new movie every six months or so. And know what?" He leaned close to Elizabeth, as if he were about to share some deep, dark secret with her.

"What?" Elizabeth asked curiously.

"They say he does all his own stunts," Bruce whispered.

"Oh." Somehow Elizabeth had expected

something a little more—well, interesting.

On the screen a man was driving a motorcycle directly into the path of an oncoming freight train, while a helicopter dropped out of the sky toward the exact spot where they would collide. Elizabeth tensed, waiting for the crash.

"Cool!" Bruce remarked, stuffing his mouth with popcorn. "Now get ready. Everything's gonna explode."

The screen filled with a huge fiery red cloud, complete with deafening sound effects. Elizabeth shuddered.

"So they're all dead," Bruce went on with obvious delight. "Except one lone man. Him." He jabbed his finger at the screen. In the corner of the wreckage, Arnold Weissenhammer began to run away from the burning disaster area.

"He's going to get the villain," Bruce said, his mouth full. "He's got, like, three broken legs, but it won't slow *him* down."

Elizabeth considered asking how someone could have three broken legs, but then she decided she didn't really want to know. "Have you seen this preview before, Bruce?"

"Maybe five times," Bruce told her. "Doesn't matter, though. They're all pretty much alike. That's what makes Weissenhammer so incredibly great."

Elizabeth sighed and snuggled closer to Bruce. She wasn't enjoying the coming attractions much, but maybe the movie would be better.

After all, she liked Bruce, and Bruce liked this kind of movie, so she must like this kind of movie too.

Right?

"There they are," Todd hissed, practically dragging Jessica into the darkened theater. In front of him he could see Elizabeth's head silhouetted against the Ultimate Jerk's shoulder. "Hurry!" he whispered.

"Hang on," Jessica said. "I want to get some popcorn."

"No time!" Todd hustled Jessica down the aisle and into the middle of the row behind Elizabeth and Public Enemy Number One. The opening credits rolled, and Arnold Weissenhammer's powerful body appeared on the screen. But Todd barely noticed. There was Elizabeth right in front of him, and—

His blood boiled. He wished he had a body like Arnold's. Then he could take Mr. Know-it-all and bend him in his bare hands.

Jessica poked Todd. "I *am* going to get some popcorn."

"OK!" Who needed popcorn at a time like this? Todd leaned forward and stared at the couple in front of him. He was so close, he could have memorized every hair on Elizabeth's head.

Keep your hands off her, you big ape, he thought.

And he wasn't talking to Arnold Weissenhammer.

"So, um, Elizabeth?" Bruce asked, sliding his hand into hers.

Elizabeth wrinkled her nose. Bruce's hand was awfully oily. *Must be from the popcorn,* she thought. She herself hadn't had much—maybe three bites.

She gripped his hand firmly, or at least as firmly as she could considering the oil. "Yes?" she asked. Behind her she could hear someone breathing hard, but she didn't turn around.

Bruce's voice was husky. "How come you like me so much, huh?"

There hadn't been a car crash in at least three minutes. Elizabeth lifted her eyes from the screen and considered. "Well—um—I mean—"

"Aw, don't be shy," Bruce said, leaning a little closer. "I've heard it all before."

"It's not that I'm shy," Elizabeth whispered back. "It's just that—" She frowned. The trouble was, she couldn't think of any reasons why she especially liked Bruce.

Oh, there were reasons, of course. She was sure of that. There had to be, since she was there with him. And she really did like him, she was sure of that too. Even if she couldn't remember exactly why.

"Because you're *you*," Elizabeth said at last, gripping Bruce's hand even harder and flashing him her most brilliant smile—just as three aircraft carriers, an armored tank, and a hospital exploded in glorious full color on the screen.

I don't believe this, Todd told himself. *I absolutely do not believe this!*

He couldn't bear to look, but of course he did anyway. Elizabeth was staring dreamily at Bruce's face, and Bruce's lips were puckered, and they were leaning closer and closer and—

Seizing Jessica's bucket of popcorn, Todd smeared a fistful of buttery kernels into Bruce's hair. Then he poured the rest of the oily stuff all over El Grosso's so-called head.

"Hey, man!" Bruce snapped, turning back. His eyes grew big when he recognized Todd.

"Oh, jeez," Todd said in a singsongy voice. "A little spill."

"What's the big idea?" Jessica sprang up from her seat. "That stuff costs money, Todd, in case you didn't know!"

"I'm going to have you arrested, you little jerk!" Bruce threatened, one extremely oily hand grabbing Todd by the collar. "Look what you've done!"

"I never would have expected you to act like an immature loser, Todd!" Elizabeth shook her head sadly. "I guess I was just plain wrong. Ignore him, Bruce. Let's watch the movie in peace."

An immature loser! Todd's mouth felt dry. Hypnotized or not, he couldn't believe Elizabeth was talking to him like that.

A pair of unoily hands grabbed him. "OK, kids." The voice—and the hands—belonged to the security guard. "Let's take this argument someplace else. We have customers here who want to see the film."

"I—I—," Todd stammered.

But it was too late. He was on his way out the door.

Actually, what happened in the theater was pretty neat, Jessica reflected as Todd stomped off to call his dad. She smiled to herself. Hypnosis sure had an amazing effect!

But still—

Jessica dropped her eyes to the ground. What had happened in the theater hadn't been exactly what she'd had in mind.

She watched from a distance as Todd punched buttons on the pay phone, so hard she thought they'd break. Once again, she felt a tiny twinge of guilt. She hadn't meant to make Todd miserable, even if he was a drip. And she hadn't meant to have her sister fall for Bruce Patman, who was really kind of a jerk when you came right down to it. It was pretty nauseating to watch them together. And that limo had been sort of over the top too. Especially because she herself hadn't gotten to ride in it.

She took a deep breath.

Now that she thought about it, she wondered if maybe she'd gone just a teeny bit too far.

Ten

◇

"Oh, Jessica, were you and Elizabeth *really* born four minutes apart?" Amy asked. "That's so cool! Because—"

"Because Amy and I were born just exactly four minutes apart too!" Janet cut in, finishing Amy's sentence.

Amy squeezed Janet's hand. "I just love being identical twins. Don't you?"

Jessica bit into her cheese and crackers savagely. It was Monday, and she was at the Unicorner, the Unicorns' usual table in the cafeteria. But the Unicorner looked different than usual.

For starters, there was Amy. Amy wasn't a Unicorn and had never even been invited to join. But now there she was, giggling with Janet as if she really *were* Janet's identical twin.

"But Janet," Lila said, "you guys don't look alike."

Janet caught Amy's eye, and they laughed again. "You're just jealous," Amy announced, "because you aren't lucky enough to have an identical twin."

Jessica sighed. She'd had hopes that morning that everyone would have come to their senses. Maybe hypnosis had some kind of a time limit or something. But Elizabeth was still completely moony about Bruce, and Janet and Amy were still convinced that they were identical twins.

It's fun having power, she reflected, biting into another cracker. *But it's more fun if you actually arrange the whole thing, instead of it all being kind of a mistake.*

"I agree with Lila," Ellen said. "You two don't look anything alike."

"Yeah, right," Janet said, waving her hand dismissively at Ellen. "See how we even wore identical—"

"Clothes?" Amy finished for her.

Jessica rolled her eyes. She and Elizabeth practically never wore the same clothes, but there were Amy and Janet, dressed in identical purple sweaters, identical white T-shirts, and identical blue jeans, with identical purses slung across their shoulders.

Lila frowned. "Just because you wear identical clothes doesn't mean you're identical twins," she protested.

"Silly old Lila," Janet said affectionately. "I told you, Amy, she's just—"

"Jealous," Amy finished.

"But—" Ellen began. She looked from one face to the other, puzzled. "You guys are teasing, right?" she asked uncertainly. "I mean, of course you're not identical twins. Why don't you cut it out already?"

"Yeah, Janet," Lila put in. "It was funny for a little while. Like, maybe, two minutes. But it's really lame by this time."

"What's she talking about?" Amy asked, raising an eyebrow.

"Beats me." Janet shrugged. "Of *course* we're identical twins."

"Have been all our lives," Amy said grandly.

"And guess who I'm taking to see the incredibly hot gymnasts at the circus on Saturday," Janet said.

Jessica smiled. She'd almost forgotten. "That's right, Janet," she said. "What time should I—"

"Not *you*," Janet said, squeezing Amy's hand. "I invited—"

"Her twin sister, of course!" Amy finished.

"But—" Jessica's hand flew to her mouth. She couldn't believe her ears.

"Well, of course, Jessica." Janet looked down her nose. "I mean, what's the point of having an identical twin sister if you don't invite her to the circus?"

Great, Jessica thought, staring down into her lunch. The idea of Amy and Janet playing twins at the circus—at *her* circus—was faintly revolting. *"Look at that gorgeous one," Amy would say, pointing at one of the gymnasts. "Dibs on him!" But Janet would just smile and say, "No, we'll both go out with him, because we're identical twins!" And then Amy would giggle and—*

Jessica tightened her mouth. *This is way past being a joke,* she thought. She wished that were all it was. But she knew better. She felt a knot in the pit of her stomach, and she suddenly wished for the old Janet back—the bossy, obnoxious Janet who ruled the Unicorns with an iron hand, not this Janet who was only interested in being Amy's twin.

"Look, Jessica!" Amy pointed to the other side of the cafeteria. "Isn't that your sister?"

Across the room Jessica could see Elizabeth walking arm in arm with Bruce. "Yeah," Jessica admitted. The knot in her stomach tightened. Elizabeth was looking adoringly at Bruce, who was suavely patting her hand.

This isn't the way it was supposed to happen, Jessica thought dismally. *She was supposed to be following me around like a little puppy dog.* She squeezed her eyes shut and imagined Elizabeth the way she'd planned her to be after the hypnosis: Elizabeth carrying her books, Elizabeth doing her homework for her (especially the hard math problems), Elizabeth picking only the TV shows Jessica wanted to watch . . .

Jessica bit her lip. Now that she thought about it, she decided it didn't sound that interesting after all. After a little while it might get kind of old.

"Hey, Jessica?" Amy asked. "I've always wondered why—"

"You and your sister don't do more stuff together," Janet finished. "Like us!"

"Because—" Jessica hesitated. *Because being identical twins doesn't mean being exactly alike,* she wanted to say. But she didn't. They'd just laugh and say, "Isn't she silly!" Or, "She has no idea what being a *real* twin is all about!"

"Oh, forget it," Jessica grumbled.

"She has no idea—" Janet said with a sly grin.

"What being a *real* twin is all about!" Amy chirped.

Jessica decided she was very quickly getting tired of being around Janet and Amy.

"Bruce?" Elizabeth asked. She was in a corner of the cafeteria, listening as Bruce discussed baseball with Aaron and Ken.

"But, you know, the Cubs aren't exactly going to the World Series this year, if you catch my drift," Bruce was saying as he swallowed an especially large bite of peanut-butter sandwich.

Elizabeth cleared her throat. "Bruce?"

"Well, if they only had some *players,*" Ken said, gesturing with a fork.

Aaron took a sip of milk and let a few drops dribble down his chin. "It isn't the *players* exactly, it's mostly the *pitching.*"

"Excuse me, Bruce?" Elizabeth tried again.

Bruce leaned forward to rest his elbows on the table, ignoring Elizabeth. "It's like I always say, work on pitching first," he insisted. "It's the same in basketball. If you don't have the guy with the three-point shot, you're nowhere."

Elizabeth sighed. She was annoyed that Bruce was being so rude. *First he invites me to have lunch with him, then he totally ignores me.* But she really, really liked him, so she wasn't going to complain too much.

It would never do to offend your own boyfriend.

Jessica tossed away the rest of her apple. The conversation in the Unicorner was leaving a bad taste in her mouth.

Janet and Amy had been rattling on and on about their shared fifth birthday party. Nobody else had gotten a word in edgewise. When Ellen had finally blown up and said, "Hey, guys, like, nobody *cares*," they'd just turned to each other and giggled.

Jessica rolled her eyes. If there was one thing Janet Howell was most definitely not, it was a giggler.

"Remember how incredibly cute those matching pink dresses were?" Amy asked.

"I'll never forget it!" Janet's eyes danced. "And we wore them to ballet class, but the teacher—"

"Wouldn't let us," Amy went on. "But luckily we had those—"

"Hot pink tutus," Janet interrupted. "Just imagine! Hot pink!" She doubled over, laughing uproariously. Amy joined her.

Jessica banged her glass down on the tray. Twins who never were. She was glad she and Elizabeth weren't such complete dorks. *Anyway,* she thought, *I like Elizabeth better being different from me. I like her the way she is.*

She glanced across to Bruce's table. Her sister was there, practically in Bruce's lap, hanging on his every word. Elizabeth and Bruce, together at last.

Whether they wanted to be or not.

Jessica sighed. *I liked my sister better the way she was B.H.—before hypnosis.*

"And the look on that teacher's face!" Amy laughed.

Jessica gritted her teeth. She couldn't escape the sneaking feeling that somehow all this was her own fault. "I wish I'd never done this," she hissed, leaning close to Lila.

Lila frowned. "Done what?"

Jessica gestured toward Amy and Janet. "This," she said with a scowl. "Hypnotized them." *There ought to be an on-off switch*, she thought. *Just push a button, and bang! The spell would be broken, just like that.*

Lila's eyebrows shot up. "Hypnotized them? You're kidding me, right?"

Jessica shook her head. "I hypnotized them into thinking they were twins," she admitted sadly.

Lila hooted. "No way. They're faking it. I'm positive. Watch the way Janet's trying to hold back a grin."

"You're wrong, Lila," Jessica said. "I really wish I hadn't done it, but—"

"You tried to hypnotize me too," Lila went on smugly, "and you, like, totally blew it." She snickered. "Remember that night at my house?"

"All right, break it up," a cheerful voice rang out. Jessica bit back an angry retort as Mr. Clark came through the cafeteria. "We don't throw food here, kids."

Mr. Clark! Jessica stiffened. Suddenly she remembered the other person she'd hypnotized—whether that other person believed it or not. She sat back in her seat. This was going to be good.

Lila stood up on her seat and waved frantically for the principal's attention.

"Mr. Quack!" she shouted happily.

"Speaking of basketball, where's Wilkins?" Ken asked.

Bruce waved his hand dismissively. "Wilkins? We had a little, um, disagreement." He poked Elizabeth in the ribs. "I don't think we'll be seeing much of him for a while."

Wilkins. Elizabeth bit her lip and frowned. Todd Wilkins, who had been such a jerk the other night in the movie theater.

But for some reason she couldn't figure out, her heart was beating faster than usual.

"It's every man for himself," Bruce said, putting his arm around Elizabeth and squeezing her tightly. "That's the way it is in the world, guys. Take it from ol' Bruce." He winked at Elizabeth. "And what can I say? Yours truly gets the goods."

Aaron frowned. "I hear you," he said slowly. "It's just that, well, you know . . ." He scratched his ear. "After what he was saying the last time we played ball . . ." His voice trailed off.

"Charm wins out in the end," Bruce remarked.

"Some of us have it, and Wilkins—well—" He shrugged elaborately.

Wilkins. That name again. Elizabeth snuggled closer to Bruce, wondering why her heart was suddenly beating even faster.

Mr. Clark frowned up at Lila. To Jessica's delight, he'd crossed over to the Unicorner when Lila yelled to him. "I beg your pardon?"

Lila grinned. "Quack, quack, Mr. Quack," she quacked.

Mr. Clark's hand went self-consciously to his head. He glared at Lila over the top of his thick glasses. "Is this some kind of a joke, young lady?"

"Quack," Lila agreed nervously. She fluttered her arms like a duck's wings.

Mr. Clark stared around at the rest of the girls in the Unicorner. "Is this another one of your silly Unicorn stunts? Because if it is—"

Oops. Jessica hadn't considered that the Unicorns might be blamed for Lila's stupid tricks. For a split second she regretted having hypnotized her friend.

But only for a split second.

"It's not a Unicorn stunt at all," Jessica said dismissively. "It's just Lila, Mr. Qu—um, Clark."

Mr. Clark tapped his foot against the tiled floor. "Lila, is this true?"

"Quack," Lila said. There was a scared look in her eyes. "Quack, quack, quack!"

Mr. Clark's eyes flashed. "That does it, young lady. I don't know what game you're playing, but—"

Lila quacked miserably.

Mr. Clark stuck out his forefinger toward her. "Detention," he ordered. "In my office. Now!"

Lila clamped her lips shut, but from the depths of her throat came a noise that sounded vaguely like a quack. Looking like she might cry, she got up slowly and left the table.

"And as for you," Mr. Clark said, pursing his lips and jabbing his finger at the girls huddled around the table, "I don't believe you're so innocent."

Janet stared at Mr. Clark in bewilderment. "Honest we are, Mr. Clark."

"We didn't know a thing," Jessica put in virtuously. "She just, like, flipped."

"It's weird, all right," Ellen added. "But it's not the Unicorns' fault, believe me."

Mr. Clark narrowed his eyes. "It's not like you have a great track record, you know."

"But we're innocent!" Jessica insisted. *He wouldn't really punish us because of what Lila did, would he?* she asked herself nervously. "I mean, we were just sitting here," she went on, casting her hand out toward her lunch, "eating cheese and crackers, and suddenly—"

"What's that you said?" Mr. Clark bellowed.

"Eating cheese and crackers," Jessica repeated, puzzled.

"That does it!" Mr. Clark glared down at her. "Detention for all the Unicorns, and extra detention for you, young lady."

"But—" Jessica's head spun. She stared down at the food in front of her.

"No buts, Miss Wakefield," Mr. Clark said as he strode purposefully away. "I've had it up to here with ducks today! I'll see you in my office."

Jessica didn't dare look at any of her friends. *It must be something I said—but what?* she thought.

Slowly she cleaned up her place. *Cheese and crackers . . . cheese and crackers . . .*

She gave a sudden groan. Mr. Clark must have thought she'd said "cheese and *quackers*"!

"Great, Jessica," Janet snapped. "Just great."

"Now we're all in trouble, and it's your fault," Amy added.

Jessica bit her lip. Nothing was going right. Most of the people she'd tried to hypnotize had been hypnotized, but the wrong way, and much as she'd wanted revenge on Lila, she hadn't really meant it to work quite the way it had. Her head spun. Maybe it was time for some professional advice.

Dr. Q isn't going to be happy if I go see her again, Jessica told herself. Head down, she walked away from the now quiet Unicorner toward Mr. Clark's office.

But what choice do I have?

Eleven

◇

Detention! Jessica wished she'd never heard of the word. She'd had to stay after school, doing stupid community service stuff, and now it was past five—too late to go see Dr. Q at her office. All because of Lila and her stupid quacking.

No. Scratch that. All because of—

Jessica sighed.

All because of her stupid idea to hypnotize everyone just to prove that she could.

Well, she'd call and leave a message. Grabbing the yellow pages, Jessica wondered what heading Dr. Q might be listed under. Psychics? Hypnotists? Inner-power tappers?

Frowning, Jessica started to page through the book.

*   *   *

"I'm home, Mom!" Jessica sprang through the door on Tuesday afternoon. She was sure Dr. Q had returned her call. "Any messages?"

"Messages?" Mrs. Wakefield looked up from a sheaf of papers. "Not for you, sweetheart."

"Oh." Jessica gulped. How could Dr. Q not have called her back? She had certainly left a frantic enough message on her answering machine the night before—unless "If you don't call me first thing tomorrow morning and tell me what to do, I'm going to die" wasn't frantic enough. "Oh," she said again.

"Is there a problem?" Mrs. Wakefield asked.

Jessica took a deep breath. "Not really," she said, but her heart was beating furiously.

How can Dr. Q ignore me like this?

If she were really psychic, she'd know I was in trouble, Jessica told herself as she angrily spun the dial to her locker Wednesday at lunch. Come to think of it, it was kind of strange for a psychic to have an answering machine.

Well, if there wasn't a call from Dr. Q by the time she got home that afternoon, she'd just have to go over to the office herself.

Things were getting worse, that was for sure. Janet had announced that the unicorn was an inappropriate symbol for their club, since the unicorn had only one horn. That was unfair to girls with identical twins, Janet insisted. Such as herself and Amy. From now on the club was going to be called the Cows.

Meanwhile, Elizabeth had told Jessica that the front page of the next *Sixers* issue would be devoted to Bruce Patman, with the headline "The Greatest All-Around Guy in SVMS History." And as for Lila, she'd been so embarrassed about the duck episode that she hadn't shown her face in school for two days.

Jessica grabbed her notebook and shoved her locker door shut with a bang.

"If I can't get hold of Dr. Q," she muttered to no one in particular, "we're all going to be in big trouble."

Big, big *trouble!*

Jessica's heart hammered as she approached the hypnotist's office on Thursday afternoon.

Six answering machine messages. At least thirty-five more messages sent via ESP. And still no word.

She pushed open the big, heavy outer door and rang the bell. *Be there*, she commanded in her mind. *Be there!*

But no one came.

Fighting a sense of panic, Jessica leaned against the bell and pushed it hard with her right thumb. Through the walls she could hear its shrill, constant ringing.

Still no one answered.

Slowly Jessica released her thumb. It was clear that Dr. Q had abandoned her in her time of need. Jessica squeezed her eyes tightly shut as a shiver of fear ran through her.

Because if Dr. Q wasn't available, then she'd have to do something about the problem herself.

*   *   *

"This demonstration better be good," Amy told Jessica on Friday night. She and Janet stood in the Wakefield rec room, wearing identical pale blue sweatshirts with the same red bow in their hair. "We have to go home and plan what we're going to wear to the circus tomorrow."

Janet blinked rapidly. "After all, we *are* identical twins."

"I know, I know," Jessica murmured, biting her nail. She was more nervous than she could ever remember being in her entire life, and Janet and Amy and their stupid games weren't helping at all.

It had been hard work getting Lila, Amy, and Janet to come to her house on such short notice, but she hoped it would all be worth it. She crossed her fingers. Then she crossed her toes too, just in case.

Lila raised one eyebrow. "If you think you can prove to all of us how psychic you really are, then you've got another thing coming."

"I can't hang around either, Jess," Elizabeth said. "Bruce might call at any moment."

Bruce! Jessica bit back a retort. If she never heard that name again in her life, it would be too soon. "OK," she said, lighting the candles and turning off the lights. "Look deep into my—"

"*And the White Sox take a three-to-one lead,*" an electronic voice blared from upstairs.

Steven! Great. Jessica darted to the door that led to the stairs. "Steven, is that you?" she shouted over the noise of her brother's ball game. "Turn the TV down! Please!"

"*Next up is the third baseman.*" The announcer's voice was as loud as ever.

"Jessica." Janet folded her arms and narrowed her mouth. "If you're just going to yell at Steven—"

Jessica made a quick decision. She'd just have to ignore the baseball game, that was all. "OK, OK," she grumbled, slamming the door shut. She crossed to the front of the room. "Look deep into my eyes."

Because if you don't, she thought to herself over Steven's broadcast, *I'll be miserable for the rest of my life!*

"Look deep into my eyes," Jessica commanded again.

Elizabeth sighed. She was tired of Jessica's silly games. *Hypnotism! Yeah, right.* She smiled to herself, remembering that Bruce was due to call soon. *Bruce the great. Bruce the wise and powerful . . .*

She yawned.

"When I say the word *wake,* you will come out of your trance," Jessica said.

But Elizabeth wasn't really listening. She yawned again.

Good thing she'd found Bruce.

Even if sometimes she couldn't imagine what in the world a totally rad guy like Bruce saw in a kid like . . . like . . . her . . .

Well, it's a start anyway, Jessica told herself. The ball game was continuing to blare, but at least all four kids in front of her looked as though they were out.

"If you are all asleep, raise your right hands," she commanded. Four right arms shot into the air. Jessica mopped her forehead, feeling a little better. She turned to Amy and Janet.

"Amy and Janet," she ordered, "forget that you were ever identical twins."

"*Oh!*" the announcer shouted on Steven's broadcast upstairs. "*The shortstop just plain forgets to cover second!*"

Jessica ground her teeth, but Amy and Janet hadn't stirred. "Elizabeth!" she said sharply, wondering how to phrase this one. "Um—you can't stand Bruce Patman."

"*The pitcher looks to the catcher for his sign—*"

"And as for you, Lila," Jessica went on, "you won't be able to think of ducks when you see Mr. Clark. No matter how hard you try."

"*Foul ball, back out of play—*"

Jessica swallowed hard. It was the moment of truth. "If you have heard me, raise your left hand," she said.

Janet thrust her left hand high in the air. "Home! Home! Get him at home!" she shouted, climbing up on her chair.

"*Pea*nuts, get yer *pea*nuts," Lila sang out. "*Crack*erjack, *pea*nuts, *pop*corn! Fresh and hot!"

"Pow! Base hit!" Amy cried, swinging an imaginary bat. "Pow! Triple to right field! Pow! Double to center! Pow!"

"The runner takes his lead off second base," Elizabeth said. "Here's the pitch—"

"*Crack*erjack!" Lila cupped her hands to her mouth and hollered louder. "Get yer *pea*nuts here!"

The blood drained from Jessica's face. *It's the baseball game,* she realized. Somehow her commands had gotten all mixed up with Steven's baseball game!

"Pow!" Amy yelled. "Single to left! Pow! Double to right!"

Jessica bit her lip so hard it hurt. Furious, she dodged past Janet, who was throwing an imaginary baseball, and flung open the door. "Steven!" she shouted. "Turn that thing off!"

"Huh?" Steven's voice sounded distant. "Says who?"

"Says me!" Jessica shrieked. "Turn it off before I—"

"Before you what?" Steven shot back.

Before I hypnotize you, Jessica thought angrily. *And come to think of it, why not?* "You are getting sleepy!" she called up the stairs, hoping she could yell over the din of the game. "When I stamp my foot, you will do whatever I say!"

There was the sound of muffled laughter from upstairs.

Jessica saw red. She could have ripped her brother limb from limb. "You are in my power!" she screamed, bringing her foot down on the bare floor with all of her might. "You have never even *heard* of baseball!"

"Huh?" Steven screamed back. "Are you out of your mind?"

"And there's a hard-hit ball to deep short," the announcer intoned. Or maybe it was Elizabeth, announcing her own private game. Jessica wasn't sure.

"You have never even *heard* . . ." Jessica's voice trailed off. She clenched her fists and let them fall to her sides. Obviously nothing was happening to Steven. It wasn't possible to hypnotize people from a distance. At least, *she* couldn't do it. "Just turn it down to a normal volume, please!"

"What?" Steven shrieked.

"Back to normal!" Jessica screamed with what felt like her last ounce of strength. And to her surprise, Steven switched the volume down. The echo seemed to ring in her ears, but for the first time in a while, Jessica could hear again.

She sighed deeply. "That noise was loud enough to wake the dead," she said, enjoying the sound of her own voice in the suddenly quiet room—

Wait a minute.

Why was the room so quiet? The other girls had been making their share of noise too, hadn't they? Jessica jerked her head up—and started in surprise.

Each of the four girls was stretching and blinking, as though she'd just awakened from a long nap.

"Gee, I want to get out of here," Elizabeth said, smiling brightly at her sister. "It's late, and I've got to meet Todd at Casey's."

Todd? Todd! Hardly daring to breathe, Jessica

stared in astonishment at her twin. Somehow the hypnosis must have worked despite the ball game.

"Ugh!" Janet shuddered and looked at Amy. Her upper lip curled. "Why are *you* dressed like *me?*" She made a face at Lila as she gestured at Amy.

"I—I—" Amy flicked her eyes back and forth from herself to Janet. "I didn't—I wouldn't—"

It looked as if everyone were back to normal— somehow. "Um, Lila?" Jessica asked, almost afraid to hear the answer. "What's the name of, you know, the principal?"

"What are you talking about?" Lila asked, sounding genuinely puzzled. "Mr. Clark, of course."

Yes! Jessica exulted. Four for four. She couldn't be prouder.

Elizabeth stood up and stretched. "You know, it seemed a little loud in here a minute ago," she said thoughtfully.

"Loud?" Jessica made a face. "Oh, that was just our beloved brother and his stupid baseball game."

"Baseball?" Elizabeth frowned. "What's that?"

"Yeah, what's baseball, Jessica?" Janet asked, rolling the word around her tongue as if it were a foreign language.

Four pairs of eyes bore in curiously on Jessica.

"Um—you know, baseball?" Jessica asked, pantomiming swinging a bat, the way Amy had been doing just a few minutes earlier. "Baseball. It's, like, baseball. You're joking, right?"

"Baseball?" Lila shook her head. "Volleyball, sure. Even basketball."

"And football," Elizabeth said. "But not baseball."

Jessica bit her lip. Her mind flashed back to the conversation she'd been yelling with Steven. Somehow the answer had to be there. What had she said, exactly?

"When I stamp my foot, you will do whatever I say." The words came crashing back at her with the force of a tidal wave. She'd thought she was hypnotizing Steven—but she wasn't.

She was rehypnotizing the four girls!

"You have never even heard of baseball!" was what Jessica had yelled up the stairs. But the other girls had heard it too—and because they were still hypnotized, they'd obeyed her command.

Jessica wished she'd gotten one command right, just for a change. But then again, not knowing about baseball wasn't such a big deal after all.

"Maybe it has something to do with music," Elizabeth said to Amy in a doubtful tone of voice. "You know, like a bass guitar or something?"

Jessica smiled faintly. What a powerful tool hypnosis could be in the hands of a true believer. In the hands of a totally psychic person. In the hands of a person like—

But at that very moment the doorbell rang.

Twelve

◇

For the first time in several days, Amy's head felt
clear. She followed Jessica toward the front door,
thinking hard. She was at the Wakefield house, that
much was for sure. Though why she was dressed
in exactly the same ridiculous outfit as Janet
Howell, she couldn't imagine for the life of her.

It wasn't as though she and Janet were bosom
buddies or anything, after all.

Amy cast her mind back. *Something about hypnosis,
maybe?* She shook her head. The last thing she remembered, she'd been down in the rec room letting Jessica
hypnotize her. *That's right. Something about flying.*

Amy's stomach took a sudden left turn. *Flying.
Ugh!*

She shivered, willing what was in her stomach
to stay there. Well, obviously Jessica's hypnosis

tricks hadn't worked. She was still as chicken about flying as ever.

And what in the world was Jessica talking about? She kept muttering something about "bait-ball." Or "basheball" or "batheball."

Jessica pulled open the door—and stared blankly into the face of Dr. Q herself.

"Good evening," Dr. Q said. She emerged from the shadows, wrapped in a blue-green robe, a frown on her face. "I know you weren't expecting me, but I just got back to town and heard your messages on my machine." She looked Jessica straight in the eye. "I thought perhaps I'd better stop by."

"Oh. Um, yeah." Jessica found it difficult to meet the psychic's unwavering gaze. She decided to play it cool. After all, she'd just convinced herself that she hadn't done the girls any harm. *They don't know about baseball,* she told herself, *but they'll learn. And otherwise they're back to normal.* "I don't need you," she said breezily. "No problemo. Piece of cake."

Dr. Q's eyes bored sternly into Jessica's own. "You were in over your head," she said.

Flustered, Jessica brushed a lock of hair from her eyes. "No, that's not it at all," she said with a laugh. "I thought I'd messed up, but I fixed it. We just had a ball down there," she added, snapping her fingers to show how very simple it was.

"Jessica?" Janet scratched her head. "Speaking of

balls, what's this baseball stuff you keep talking about?"

Jessica wet her lips nervously. "Um—"

"And how come I'm still scared of helicopters?" Amy demanded.

Dr. Q looked from Amy to Janet and back, shaking her head. "As I suspected," she said dryly. "Didn't I tell you that hypnosis is not a toy?"

"But—" Jessica bit her lip. "They're—they're back to normal, Dr. Q, I'm telling you—"

"Jessica." Dr. Q's voice was soft but firm.

Jessica looked at the ground.

"Hey!" Steven's head appeared over the railing. "Home run for the Angels! But the White Sox still lead, seven to three."

"Since when do angels run home?" Amy wanted to know.

Steven scowled. "They're *teams*, you clowns. *Baseball* teams, duh."

"Baseball." Elizabeth looked puzzled. "So you know about Jessica's new game too?"

"Huh?" Steven shook his head. "Oh, forget it," he remarked, and disappeared.

"Baseball." Janet laughed her high-pitched laugh again, and Lila joined in. "Now, if I were inventing a new sport, I'd call it something way cooler than baseball. Unicornball, maybe."

"Jessica." Dr. Q's voice seemed firmer than ever, and Jessica knew what she had to do.

She took a deep breath. "I'm, um, sorry," she admitted, not quite daring to look Dr. Q in the face. "You did tell me that hypnosis wasn't a toy. And I didn't really try to use it that way," she said defensively.

Dr. Q lifted an eyebrow the merest fraction of an inch.

Jessica twisted her hands. "All right, all right," she said vehemently. "But I didn't mean it. I was going to help Amy and Janet be less scared, and I was going to—um—" She decided not to let Dr. Q know what she'd planned for Elizabeth and Lila.

"I see." Dr. Q nodded slowly.

"So could you—" Jessica paused, afraid to ask the question. But she knew, deep down, that she had no choice. "Could you do one last, I mean *really* last, hypnosis for us, Dr. Q? Could you help these guys remember what baseball is?"

"And get rid of my fear of flying?" Amy said.

I tried to do that part, Jessica told herself.

But you didn't really know what you were doing, a voice inside her head argued back.

A smile played around the corners of Dr. Q's mouth. "All right," she said at last.

And Jessica breathed a sigh of relief.

Elizabeth sat up straight and looked around. It was the old familiar rec room, and there was Jessica, and Amy, who looked like she was asleep, and Lila and Janet. And Dr. Q.

"Elizabeth?" Jessica asked nervously. "Um—finish the sentence, OK? Strike—?"

"Three," Elizabeth filled in.

Jessica managed a weak smile. "So you've heard of baseball?" she asked.

Of course she'd heard of baseball, Elizabeth thought. It was one of Steven's six or seven favorite sports. The Cardinals and the Blue Jays, bats and balls, mitts, the whole deal. She nodded.

"Center—?" Jessica looked at her twin expectantly.

"Field," Elizabeth answered.

"Batter—?" Jessica's eyes sparkled.

Elizabeth considered saying 'pancakes' just for fun, but she didn't. "Up," she said instead.

"Phew." Jessica swallowed hard and grinned. "I'm *so* glad you're back."

Lila leaned over. "Do you, like, remember anything from when you were hypnotized?"

Elizabeth watched Dr. Q talking with Amy. She thought hard. Yes, she did. She remembered not knowing about baseball. And she remembered going out with somebody strange. Somebody who wasn't Todd. With—

Her stomach sank. With Bruce Patman!

The whole awful week came suddenly flashing back at her. The night at the Weissenhammer movie, when she'd called Todd an immature loser. Her cheeks flushed at the memory. The days she'd sat with Bruce in the cafeteria, listening to him ignore her. What a fool she'd been! Her heart sank; she could see the headline in the next issue of the *Sixers*, which would go to press on Monday: "The

Greatest All-Around Guy in SVMS History."

Elizabeth's mouth felt dry. How could she have stuck with Bruce and thrown away Todd?

Lila frowned. "I said, did you remember anything about—"

"Not a single thing," Elizabeth lied, crossing her fingers behind her back and wondering how to make it up to poor old Todd, the one guy who really cared about her. "Not one single, solitary thing!"

"I hear you," Amy mumbled. Her eyelids fluttered open. Slowly she looked around the room and into the eyes of Dr. Q.

"Helicopter," Dr. Q said softly.

Amy held her breath. But the room wasn't spinning, and she wasn't feeling trapped.

"Ah." Dr. Q's voice was smooth and even. "Flying."

Amy bit her lip. There was no knot in the pit of her stomach, no frantic tightening of her throat, no suddenly sweaty palms. *Maybe I'm cured*, she thought, not daring to speak.

"You are in a helicopter," Dr. Q said. "A sudden gust of wind strikes it as it chugs through the air three thousand feet above Sweet Valley. How do you feel?"

Amy closed her eyes. Before that evening, she would have turned green and had a panic attack, no question. But now—

Now it almost sounded fun.

"Yes!" Amy shouted, springing up into the air and pumping her fist. She'd be able to do that interview after all. "It worked!" she yelled. "Let's go to Casey's and celebrate!"

"With *you* wearing *my* outfit?" Janet narrowed her eyes. "I don't think so." Her eyes flicked down to her own clothes. "Let's get out of here, Lila. You too, Jessica. The last thing we need is a Unicorn wanna-be running loose."

Amy blinked. She remembered it all now: how she and Janet had thought they were identical twins, how they'd spent every minute of every day talking, planning, and giggling, how they'd probably driven everyone crazy.

And with Janet Howell, of all people! She shook her head.

"It's OK, Janet," she said, smiling. "I'll be me, and you be you. And let's agree to have nothing in common again, ever!"

"I still can't figure it out," Todd said morosely. He beat a quarter idly against the table in front of him and sipped his chocolate milk shake. He and Ken were at a booth that evening in Casey's ice cream parlor.

Ken swallowed a bite of his sundae. "Can't figure what out?"

"E.W.," Todd said glumly. The quarter fell onto the floor, but he made no move to pick it up. What was the point? "Here I thought she, you know, liked me, and, well, maybe she did." He paused to consider. "And then her stupid sister has to go and hypnotize her into thinking she's in love with Bruce the Idiot Patman." His shoulders sagged. "You know, if she'd run off with someone like you, I could have handled that. Maybe."

"Thanks a lot." Ken rolled his eyes. "I think."

Todd didn't respond. Without Elizabeth, life seemed meaningless. *Maybe I'll quit school and just stay here in Casey's and drink milk shakes until I'm forty*, he thought. *I mean, why not?*

"It's because Patman's the original girls-stink guy," Ken said sympathetically. He jerked a thumb over his shoulder. "And don't look now, but he's sitting over there."

"Really?" Todd sat forward warily. He wondered if he should go punch Patman out. Wasn't that what they'd done back in the olden days? They challenged each other to duels, that was it. Yeah. He'd go slap Patman on both cheeks and challenge him to a duel. To the death, preferably. On the basketball court at dawn.

He stared over Ken's shoulder. There was Patman, sitting with Aaron Dallas and blowing straw wrappers all around Casey's. *Typical.* His blood boiled. Doggone it, even if Elizabeth *was* hypnotized, she should have known better than to fall for a loser like that!

Behind Bruce, the door opened, and two girls walked in. Todd doubled over as if he'd been hit in the stomach. Elizabeth and Amy. Just exactly the people he did *not* want to see, thanks very much. He started to stand up.

"Where are you going?" Ken hissed.

"Out," Todd said. "If you think I'm going to sit here and watch while she sits down with *Bruce* . . ."

Ken shook his head. "That's what Bruce wants," he explained. "Just stay and don't let it bug you, man."

Todd took a long breath and let it out slowly. He knew, deep down, that Matthews was right. The problem was that he'd put so much time into Elizabeth. He'd memorized her walk, her laugh, her favorite clothes, the way she sharpened pencils. He'd spent hours wondering what movie she'd like. Then he'd put his heart, his soul, his whole *life*, into that stupid letter inviting her to see it with him.

Well, obviously she'd been a waste of time and energy.

Too bad he couldn't take his eyes off her.

Elizabeth ordered a milk shake at the counter. Biting his lip, Todd watched Elizabeth take her purse off her shoulder in that gesture she knew so well. He saw her lips curve into that old familiar smile. He saw her pick up the shake she'd ordered and walk quickly toward Bruce's table.

"Hey, Elizabeth!" Bruce grinned. "Bet that's for me, huh?" he said, winking at Aaron.

Todd watched, cringing. He hoped that Elizabeth wouldn't actually let Bruce touch her. The thought made him shudder.

"So you wanted to show me just how much you like me, huh?" Bruce was speaking again.

Elizabeth's eyes narrowed. "That's about right,"

she said. And to Todd's astonished delight, she sloshed the entire shake into Bruce's lap.

"Hey!" Bruce sputtered, standing up and grabbing a handful of napkins.

"Thanks for a great week," Elizabeth said sarcastically. "Don't bother to call me again, OK?"

All right! Todd felt like standing up and applauding. But he didn't. Instead, he caught his breath.

Elizabeth was on her way over to his table.

What should I do? Todd's head whirled. Should he hide? Run? Stay where he was? *Why would Elizabeth want to talk to me?* he asked himself. He hoped it was because—

"Hello, Todd." Elizabeth toyed with the empty cup in her hand. "Um—I just wanted to say I was sorry."

Sorry? Todd's heart skipped a beat. He looked up at her, scarcely daring to breathe.

"I—I know I've been acting like a total jerk lately," Elizabeth went on slowly, not quite meeting Todd's eyes. "But, um, I apologize. Let's just say I haven't been myself."

Todd nodded, not trusting himself to speak.

"And—" Elizabeth paused. "I want to make it up to you." She reached into her purse and pulled out a slip of paper, which she let fall into his lap. "I hope you say yes," she said, smiling faintly.

Todd bit his lip. Slowly he unfolded the note. It was a single sheet of notebook paper. Bright orange, the kind Elizabeth had in the third section of her binder. Licking his lips nervously, he began to read.

"7:45 Fri. evening

Dear Todd,
  Hi. Writing notes is kind of awkward. Don't you think so?
  Well, I was just kind of wondering if you wanted to go to a movie. With me, I mean. Saturday night. We could go see the Eileen Thomas movie if you want. . . .

Todd grinned. It was almost identical to the note he'd written Elizabeth the week before. His eyes flicked to the end.

  "But if you don't want to, I understand.
                    Yours,
                    Elizabeth
  P.S.: Wakefield, that is"

Elizabeth reached for Todd's hand and held it. "I'm really sorry, Todd," she murmured. "Will you—will you go to the movie with me?"
  Todd could feel himself blushing, but he didn't even care.
  "Yup, I guess I could make it," he said, rising to his feet and staring into her eyes. But inside he was exulting.
  I'm going out with E.W. after all!

Thirteen

"What do you mean, I can't watch the baseball game?" Steven's eyes flashed. "It's one of the most important games of the year! If the Angels lose today, they're history! How can you tell me I can't watch the game just because of some stupid news report?"

"Because," Elizabeth said firmly. She seized the remote control and held it out of his reach. Todd sat beside her on the couch. "Amy is going to be on the air. And you can watch a baseball game any old day, but this is your only chance to see a live report from Amy Sutton, ace TV reporter." *Or maybe not the only chance,* she added to herself. She suspected that this was just the start of something big for her friend.

"Yeah," Todd agreed, gently squeezing Elizabeth's hand. He smiled at Elizabeth, and her heart soared. It was Sunday afternoon, and a bunch of kids were gathered at the Wakefields' to see Amy's report. The previous night she and Todd had finally gotten to go see the Eileen Thomas movie, and the whole evening had been as good as she could have imagined.

No. Better.

"All right." Steven scowled. "I'll go listen to it on the radio, then." He stomped off.

"Baseball." Lila laughed. "I still can't believe you hypnotized us to forget about baseball, Jessica."

"Well, there are times I'd like to forget all about it," Jessica remarked. "Like when my dear brother is trying to monopolize the TV set." She leaned forward and fiddled with the brightness knob. "It's almost time."

"Do you want to, um, go to Casey's with me after this is over?" Todd asked Elizabeth.

Elizabeth nodded happily. "There's just one thing I've got to do first," she murmured, keeping her eyes fixed on the screen.

"Which is?" Todd asked.

Elizabeth winced at the thought of the *Sixers* lead story she'd planned on Bruce Patman. No way *that* article would ever see the light of day. Dr. Q had confirmed that it wasn't hypnosis that had made Bruce ask her out; apparently he'd done it just because he was a jerk. "I have an article to write for the *Sixers*," she explained. Luckily she already knew what she was going to write: an exposé of hypnosis.

Not exactly the way she'd thought she'd write it, of course. Not after being hypnotized. In her head she could already see the lead sentence of her front-page story: *In the hands of a master psychic such as Dr. Q, hypnosis is safe, easy, and rewarding.* Something like that.

"OK." Todd wrinkled his nose. "Well, do you mind if I, you know, hang around till you're done?"

Elizabeth smiled and leaned against his shoulder.

"I don't mind a bit," she said.

Amy took a deep breath as the camera's red light glowed. She was on the air!

"This is Amy Sutton, and I'm talking with Mindy Gray, the daughter of the helicopter pilot," she said with a smile. "Mindy, how do you feel about your mom's job?"

Mindy was a short blond girl with eyes the color of her last name. She leaned forward to speak into the microphone. "I love it," she said, flashing Amy a shy smile. "I get a kick out of going up with her, and I think it's cool that she can pilot something this big."

Now that the first question was out of the way, Amy felt a little more at ease. "Are you ever frightened?" she asked.

Mindy shook her head vehemently. "No way! Why would I be frightened?" she asked as the copter swung into a turn. "It's like a whole different world up here. And anyway, a helicopter's like a car, with seat belts and everything." She laughed.

Amy laughed too. She'd never thought about that before. But it was true: A helicopter *was* a little like a car. And she'd never been frightened of driving in a car. "Some people might say it was fright-ening," she said aloud.

"Some people might," Mindy agreed. "But not me."

Amy smiled. "And not me either!" she said.

"She's doing great, isn't she?" Todd whispered as he watched the broadcast.

Elizabeth nodded. "I can't believe that she used to be totally terrified of flying. And just a couple of days ago too!"

Todd grimaced as the copter hit an air pocket and the picture jumped—but Amy didn't even seem to notice.

It all went to show what a little hypnosis could do.

He stroked Elizabeth's hand and smiled to himself.

Of course, sometimes you could get exactly what you wanted even without having to be hyp-notized. . . .

"And how about the future?" Amy asked. She knew she'd have to hurry up the last few questions. Television reporting wasn't like working on a news-paper. Everything had to be short, short, short. "What do you want to do for a living, Mindy?"

Mindy faced the camera. "When I grow up, I want to be a helicopter pilot—just like my mom."

Off in the corner Amy could see Mrs. Sutton giv-ing her the signal to end the interview. Perfect tim-ing. Grabbing the microphone, she leaned toward the camera.

"Know what, Mindy?" she asked. "After talking to you and experiencing this flight, I think I can see why!"

"This is Dyan Sutton, together with my daughter, Amy, live from three thousand feet above Sweet Valley."

Jessica stood up and stretched. "Pretty good report," she admitted. Amy hadn't seemed nervous at all.

"Yeah, it was," Lila agreed. "I just don't know why she wore that tacky sweatshirt instead of—"

"It all just goes to prove," Jessica interrupted, making sure everyone could hear her, "what hypnosis can do. If it hadn't been for me, Amy would never have been in the air." She straightened her collar. "No autographs, please."

"If it hadn't been for *you?*" Lila sounded incredulous. "Give me a break!"

"As I remember it," Elizabeth said with a smile, "it was Dr. Q who had to undo all the mischief you'd done."

"And Dr. Q who finally hypnotized Amy into not being afraid of flying," Todd pointed out.

"Yeah, well," Jessica said with a dismissive wave of her hand, "that's just details. I'd have figured out a way to get her hypnotized right. And besides, it was all everybody else's fault for talking during the hypnosis. And besides—"

"And besides, you owe me big time for all that

detention you made me do," Lila went on, staring daggers at Jessica. "I still don't know exactly how you did it, but—"

"Anyway, I have bigger and better plans now," Jessica interrupted. "Next I'm going to hypnotize my parents."

"Our parents?" Elizabeth sat up, puzzled. "Why?"

"Because I need a bigger allowance," Jessica explained.

Elizabeth shook her head. "Jessica, don't you dare!"

But Jessica only smiled.

It was funny, but deep down in her bones, she just knew that she could pull it off. Not to mention that the tarot cards had said so the previous night.

So it had to be true.

Right?

Jessica may be a great hypnotist, but Elizabeth doesn't need hypnosis to get her way in Sweet Valley Twins #103, ELIZABETH SOLVES IT ALL.

Bantam Books in the SWEET VALLEY TWINS series.
Ask your bookseller for the books you have missed.

SIGN UP FOR THE SWEET VALLEY HIGH® FAN CLUB!

Hey, girls! Get all the gossip on Sweet Valley High's® most popular teenagers when you join our fantastic Fan Club! As a member, you'll get all of this really cool stuff:

- Membership Card with your own personal Fan Club ID number
- A Sweet Valley High® Secret Treasure Box
- Sweet Valley High® Stationery
- Official Fan Club Pencil (for secret note writing!)
- Three Bookmarks
- A "Members Only" Door Hanger
- Two Skeins of J. & P. Coats® Embroidery Floss with flower barrette instruction leaflet
- Two editions of *The Oracle* newsletter
- Plus exclusive Sweet Valley High® product offers, special savings, contests, and much more!

Be the first to find out what Jessica & Elizabeth Wakefield are up to by joining the Sweet Valley High® Fan Club for the one-year membership fee of only $6.25 each for U.S. residents, $8.25 for Canadian residents (U.S. currency). Includes shipping & handling.

Send a check or money order (do not send cash) made payable to "Sweet Valley High® Fan Club" along with this form to:

SWEET VALLEY HIGH® FAN CLUB, BOX 3919-B, SCHAUMBURG, IL 60168-3919

NAME_____
(Please print clearly)

ADDRESS_____

CITY_____ STATE_____ ZIP_____
(Required)

AGE_____ BIRTHDAY_____ /_____ /_____